IN AN A[GE OF] CRUSADES, KNIGHTHOOD, LECHERY, AND GRANDILOQUENT STORYTELLING . . .

An earthy, hard-loving woman and a colorful cast of characters set off on a great pilgrimage to the Bishopric of Canterbury: the gallant Knight, the lewd Summoner, the icy Prioress, the seductive Franklyn, and many more—including the poet himself, Geoffrey Chaucer. And it is to him that a beleaguered but unbowed Wife of Bath tells the story of her love-life . . . of her husbands: the ones who hurt her, the ones who loved her well, and the ones who were worthy in their degree.

It's a no-holds-barred romp through Olde England, up to the final, delicious surprise—a miracle at Canterbury.

THE WIFE OF BATH

VERA CHAPMAN

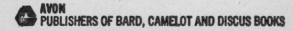

AVON
PUBLISHERS OF BARD, CAMELOT AND DISCUS BOOKS

AVON BOOKS
A division of
The Hearst Corporation
959 Eighth Avenue
New York, New York 10019

First Avon Printing, August, 1978

AVON TRADEMARK REG. U.S. PAT. OFF AND IN
OTHER COUNTRIES, MARCA REGISTRADA,
HECHO EN U.S.A.

Printed in the U.S.A.

PART ONE

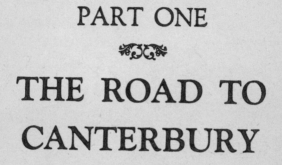

THE ROAD TO CANTERBURY

ONE

Enter Alison

"OW!" said Alison, "stop pinching me, you rogue—" as Harry Bailey, the host, handed her down from her horse in the courtyard of the *Tabard*. She was beginning to enjoy herself.

Three weeks ago it had been very different—she had been a defeated woman, a woman growing old; crouched by her daughter-in-law's fire, with a shawl over her head, beginning to be peevish and scolding. The cold got into her bones, and into her ears—one ear was quite deaf, and that was Jenkyn's legacy—and Jenkyn was dead, dear, teasing Jenkyn, the last and youngest of her five husbands, with his bitter tongue and his sweet, sweet lips. Jenkyn was dead, and she was growing old. Gilbert, her eldest son, was good to her and so was his wife Elizabeth, but she was beginning to grumble and scold at them.

"Mother," said Gilbert one day when Lent had just begun, "why don't you try another pilgrimage?"

"Hey? What?" She swung round to get his voice on her right side. "Pilgrimage? Oh God—I'm too old. Can't be plagued with pilgrimages any more. Too deaf. Keep your pilgrimages."

"No, but mother—" He settled down confidentially beside her, and drew her close to him. "You're neither too old nor too deaf—look, you can hear me quite well like this. Saint Thomas of Canterbury—do you know what I heard tell the other day? Old Will of the *Bell*, who was deaf as a gatepost, went to Canterbury last summer, and came back hearing as well as I do. And Peter Pott's aunt was cured of the scrofula, the same way; and John Jones never had another falling fit since he went there—oh, and hundreds more. Why not try Canterbury?"

"Oh me!—Boy, I've been to Compostella, and I've been to blessed Jerusalem—and I'm deafer than before. Will you tell me that Saint Thomas will do me any more good than blessed Jerusalem?"

"Oh, I don't know—anyhow, mother dear, you'd enjoy the journey—you know you always did. The ride would do you good, you know it would. Come now, why not give Saint Thomas a chance? After all, Canterbury's not so far. . . ."

She went out to the door. Once more it was "betwene March and Averil"—pale blue was showing through the clouds, and a sweetness was coming up from the earth. A blackbird flew round from her left to her right, and his song, sweet and liquid, came up to her.

Canterbury wasn't so far, and she wasn't yet so old. When she turned back to Gilbert, the smile of twenty years back was on her face, and she tossed the shawl off her head.

"Buy me a pony," she said. "I'll see what Saint Thomas can do."

And so she came riding into the courtyard of the *Tabard* on a fresh day in spring—the sixteenth of April as ever was. Alison Johnson, widow, close on fifty-one; plump and pink-cheeked, her hair a reddish-gold, sprinkled a little with grey, but mostly hidden under the fine lawn wimple that secured her broad-brimmed hat; none the less, a few blonde curls blowing about her warm cheeks. Her eyes green and wide like a surprised kitten's, her teeth still white and perfect, spaced apart and showing the "gaps" that mean a traveller; her mouth, her eyes, her bosom, her hips all wide and generous.

She rode comfortably astride of her well-padded saddle, with her big cloak spread out to cover her tucked-up skirt, though one could see her red stockings, new russet leather riding-boots and formidable spurs. No side-saddle for her! She had got herself an outfit of the very best, and took pleasure in every stitch of it. Oh, she wasn't dead yet! She grinned at the sun in the sky, at the chirruping sparrows, at the cat on the doorpost as she went into the courtyard—and squealed as Harry Bailey lifted her down. She was done with being sorry for herself, and out to enjoy the world again.

The courtyard in the late morning was animated, and fast filling up. In the long line of the stables there were already some two dozen horses—she scanned them with an experienced traveller's eye, speculating on their owners. That was a fine hefty war-horse—yes, she thought, that distinguished shabby middle-aged man, rubbing it down, he must be a Knight, for all his dingy old stable coat. That would be his son with him—what a head of golden curls, bless the lad! He'd got a fine slim-built bay, full of spirit. He'd be showing off once they got on the road. There was a couple of bony hacks—poor scholars most likely. Whose was that dainty fat palfrey, all over bells and things? Clerical, if she knew anything. And that big raw-boned roan—that must belong to a sizeable man. Oh yes, all sorts, rich and poor, clerical and lay, smart and shabby, all there. She'd met them before. No surprises. Or, well? there was always the possibility of surprises. Always men—a sixth husband? Why not?

Across the courtyard two men were singing—as far as she could see, one lanky and yellow-haired, warbling in an affected sugary tenor, and the other a great rough, dark lump of a man, harmonizing in a resonant bass. She heard them when she turned her right ear towards them, but not when she turned her left. That annoyed her.

The host came hurrying back to her. She was expected, arrangements having been made for her place in the company by her brother John's son, now in London. That was the best of a large family, it gave you kith and kin in so many places; and yet she preferred to travel alone.

Harry Bailey was a fine cheerful figure of a man, rotund and bright-eyed, and with a look of authority. This would be a good trip, she felt—this man was a capable organizer. He had stopped to exchange a word with another man as he came—one hardly so impressive as Harry, being half a head shorter, but handsome in a middle-aged way, stocky and broad-shouldered, with a well-shaped head and snow-white hair that shone; clean and well-groomed, his little neat beard trimmed to a point, like daisy-petals against the red of his cheeks. He had a countrified look, but adequate and assured; a man well adjusted to the world, comfortable, thriving, and unspoilt by his prosperity.

Alison would have liked to hear that man's voice; the accord of the voice with the face was wont to teach her a great deal about the nature of the man. But not a sound could she catch at the moment, and the white-bearded man was in a hurry and not stopping to talk.

"There's two more ladies in the party, madam," said Harry. "I feared you'd have been the only lady here—indeed I very much feared it. But fortunately they've sent word over by messenger from Stratford, and they'll soon be here. Two ladies of religion, in fact, which will be pleasant company for you."

"Eh?" she half-turned her head. "Ladies of religion? Two nuns? I don't like nuns. By the Mass, do you think I'd be afraid to ride alone with a party of men?"

"Well—" the host raised his eyebrows at her, and bent over her with a gesture of gallantry. "That is to say, madam—a lady like yourself would have nothing to fear from the likes of us—it's our pleasure. . . ." The song from the corner suddenly increased, and from the back of the stables came the rival snarl of bagpipes. "Not but what there's a few roughish customers in the party, like there always is—I tell you what, I think I'd better come with you to protect you—"

11

"Ah, go along with you," she rejoined, beaming. "You'd better come and protect the nuns. Now then, tell me, who's here?"

"Quite a company, madam—well, first, there's Sir Ralph over there, a Knight just come from the wars. A fine gentleman if there ever was one—caring for his horse before he cares for himself too. And that's his son, young Master Leonard de Bourne. Nice young fellow too. Then that gentleman over there with the white beard, he's a franklyn from Norfolk, and keeps a fine house, I'm told. Very free with his money, but puts on airs a bit, you know. See that lot over there, all in the same livery? Fine picture they make—a haberdasher, a dyer, a carpenter, a weaver and a carpetmaker. They all stick together and don't say much to the rest. That one with the forked beard and the Flemish hat, he's a merchant; there's a lawyer, too, and a doctor, and a clerk—"

"A clerk, is there?"

"Oh yes, but a sober and poor one—not one of your flighty young sparks. Sits with his eyes down and says nothing—always reading his books, and never looks up at a pretty girl. Not like some . . . and then of course there's the old Parson, too, and his brother. A quiet pair, and not much money to throw about; but good men, both of 'em. Honest as the sunlight. More than I can say of some of them—those two cater-wauling over there, now, a Summoner and a Pardoner—"

"Hum! God bless us, that's nice company. We're sure to have the devil amongst us. Any more clergy? That fat pony with the bells on?"

"Oh yes, that's a monk, and a fine figure he makes.

He does himself well and no mistake. And a friar too—he'll keep you entertained, madam—"

"Entertained? I'd as soon be entertained by Satan himself. Don't let him ride near me. Bless us, what's that noisy lot over there? Are they the two you spoke of?"

"I'm afraid, madam, they are a little—merry, as you might say. I beg you'll make allowance for them."

The two singers came lurching across the courtyard together. They presented a remarkable sight at closer view—the tall blond one, with a pink, beardless face and long, lank yellow hair draping round it like a doll's, the resemblance to which was heightened by his protuberant blue eyes. A carved church angel in a picture—but a slightly shop-soiled, raffish and dubious one, and not so innocent as an angel ought to look. His attire was semi-clerical, but he disdained to wear a cowl—instead he wore a little round black cap, perched high on his head, surmounted by a conspicuous tinsel cross containing a relic; that marked him out for a Pardoner, a peddler of holy relics and indulgences, patent medicine for all ills of the soul, here and hereafter. A smooth, holy spiv—but his companion looked a more alarming type, if more authoritative. His habit showed him to be the Archdeacon's Summoner—one with authority to bring offenders, particularly clerical ones, before the Archdeacon's Court for discipline: an office ideal for blackmail. Anyone might be afraid of such a spiritual Bow-Street Runner, even without this one's gross red face, disfigured all over with unsightly pimples and carbuncles, and further inflamed with rich living; his small, cunning eyes under scabby black brows, and his grotesque thin beard. Of all incongruous decorations, a huge round garland of flowers crowned his unlovely head, and he flourished a big flat loaf in his left hand, like a shield. He was jabbering a rich farrago of Latin tags.

"Good reverend sirs," said Harry Bailey, approaching them, "I beseech you that you'll be a little moderate—this is an honest house, and we shall have ladies in the company—"

"*Honestas, ad rerum roarum,*" said the Summoner, with great gravity. "*Moderatio est, hic! Moderatus sum—questio quid—mirabile dictu.*"

"He's drunk," said the Pardoner with equal gravity, and continued his song: "*My dainty love, my lily flower—*" and the Pardoner joined in resonantly: "*In floram doram co-o-oram. . . .*"

Harry turned from them, shrugging his shoulders. "No doing anything with them, I fear, madam. No matter—I'll sort them later. Now, as to the rest of the company. There's a cook—one Roger of Ware, a good fellow for the work, and I'm taking him with us so that we can be sure of good fare; also he wants to go to Saint Thomas to pray to be healed of an ulcer on his leg, poor fellow. He got it burnt with a hot spit once, and it's never healed. And that one with the black beard—he's a sea-captain from Dartmouth, skipper of the *Maudelayne*. Then that hefty great fellow with the bagpipes, he's a miller. I'm afraid we shall have trouble with him—quarrelsome, you know. Let me see, is that all of us? Oh no—there's Master Oswald the Reeve of Baldeswell in Norfolk—over there, the withered old fellow, all bunched up, just getting off the bay stallion. And there's a Manciple of the Temple, and of all things there's a poet."

"What, a poet? I thought they didn't go about with

common folk, but day-dreamed in their closets among books. What does he look like?''

"Oh, nothing remarkable. That little fellow over there, with the straggling grey beard and the long-ended cap. Master Geoffrey Chaucer—they say he's written a lot of high-flown stuff no one ever reads. A good thing he's got a steady job in the King's household, or he'd be as poor as the old Parson. That's the lot, I think, except for the religious ladies and their priest. Why, by the Mass, here they come.''

TWO
Enter the Prioress

THEY did indeed—a jingling of bells and bridles, a stirring and flouncing and rustling, and above all a yapping of little dogs went before them like a herald. Into the courtyard they rode—the Prioress leading, her sister-chaplain behind on her right, and on her left her attendant priest; and all the Prioress's dogs scrapping and yelping around the feet of the cavalcade.

The Prioress rode in magnificence, seated side-saddle on a beautiful white mule—her black mantle and veil serving only as a foil to the dazzling spread of her wimple around her cold, handsome face. Alison's fine linen suddenly seemed coarse and dingy beside it. The writer of the *Ancren Rule* must have had the Prioress in mind when he wrote: "Some nuns sinneth in hir wimplinge no less thanne ladie." Fold upon fold of exquisite, cobweb-fine whiteness, a snowy castle for an icy princess or the ruffling breast of a swan on a dark lake. Below it a great gold and enamel brooch, boldly devised with a blue "A," clasped her mantle; and round her left wrist, twined over her white doeskin glove, was her rosary, a costly trinket of coral and gold. And from the folds of her lap the tiniest of her dogs peeked up with its bright eyes.

The nun beside her might have been chosen for her foil—nothing could ever make that gentle, self-effacing face anything but plain. She rode with her eyes fixed on the Prioress as if to anticipate her slightest wish; and the Prioress never looked in her direction, but carried on a dignified and aloof conversation, with some restrained and seemly mirth, with her priest—a polished and courtly cleric, whose smooth and silver-powdered face carried a smile of complaisance and comfort. As the Prioress brought her mount to a standstill, he hastened to help her dismount, which she did with a graceful swirl of draperies; and so she came face to face with Alison. Their first reaction to each other's presence was as of cat and dog; then their eyes met in recognition.

"God's my life!" said Alison, "it's little neighbour Edith! Well, how do you, gossip, after all these years?"

The Prioress recoiled a little, and then advanced again upon Alison with the look of one not entirely displeased to meet an old friend who should be an appreciative witness of one's glory.

"Oh," she piped in a high and over-sugared voice, "now I do believe I recognize you, my dear woman. Ain't you little Alison Prout that used to live at the mill at Watchet?"

"I am that same," beamed Alison with deliberate

and disconcerting heartiness. "Bless thee, lass!" And she fairly fell upon the shrinking Prioress, enveloping her hand in a hot clasp and, breaking through the lawn entanglements, smacked a kiss on her cheek. "Yes, I'm Alison Johnson, was Baldwin, was Hardiman, was Watkyn, was Lucas, was Prout—at your service." The little lapdog yapped in protest, the Prioress still clutching him.

"O Saint Loy!" tittered the Prioress. "You've married much—five times, is it?"

"Five times, thank God. And you're still Edith Ditton?"

"Oh, not Edith, my dear. You must now call me Mother Eglantyne."

Alison laughed. "Eglantyne? What sort of a name is that? And 'Mother' to boot—"

The Prioress frowned. "It's my name of religion."

"Religion indeed! I never heard a name like that in the Bible. So plain Edith wasn't good enough for you." She stood back and looked at her critically. "Well, you always wanted to do it, and you have. I hope you like it."

"What do you mean, my dear?" The Prioress put on a voice of sweet and martyred tolerance. "The life of religion? I have my vocation, and it is all my love and liking. Stop barking, Troilus. It is the only life of peace and happiness, my dear. *Your* life, now—you must have suffered much. The years have taken their toll of you."

"Oh, not so much of that either," said Alison, flouncing. "I've had my ups and downs, and you're looking your age too, if you come to that."

"Oo! *Pardonny-moy*," said the Prioress, with a

shocked upward toss of her hands, and a plain and downright English accent.

"*Pardonnez-moi,*" retorted Alison, with a deep curtsey, in an accent that was French enough for the gutters of Paris—and followed it up with an expression Rabelais would have approved. The Prioress looked blank, then noticed the bystanders sniggering. Her face reddened.

"We don't speak *that* kind of French," she said, "at Stratford-atte-Bow."

As she turned away curtseying ironically to Alison, who curtseyed back again at her, there was a shout and a sound of fury, and from the door of the inn came flying a small dog, bunched together in fright and yelping—then a boot, then various household articles, and lastly Mrs. Harry Bailey, flourishing a stick, and shouting her anger to the high heavens, telling the world in good plain English what the dog had done.

The Prioress gave a ladylike shriek.

"Oh, my sweet Sweeting! Come to mother, then—," and dropping the discomfited lap-dog, she gathered the fugitive up into her bosom.

"Sweeting, you call that filthy imp of hell?" vociferated the landlady, and proceeded to enlarge on the situation. The Prioress stood like a lioness defending its young.

"Oh, but my poor innocent Sweeting—what has he done?"

The landlady told her.

"And you beat him? With that great stick?—Oh, you cruel, wicked woman!" And Madam Eglantyne burst into tears and sobbed like a child, fondling and kissing the disgraced Sweeting. Dame Bailey went on shouting, protesting that she wouldn't have one of the filthy hounds in her clean house—but the Prioress, as the best method of defence, paid no attention to her but continued to weep, her sobs and shrieks growing so alarmingly hysterical that her attendant nun and the priest had to lead her gently away—the nun carefully rounding up the rest of the dogs—and the party retired in good order, with, on the whole, the honours of war—leaving the enemy vociferating alone.

Alison stood and watched this scene with detached enjoyment. Only—

"God's pity!" she said to herself—"I shall have to sleep with that lot!"

Supper was a noisy cheerful meal. Alison found herself seated by the Prioress, greatly to her disgust, but apparently the host thought it fitting that the only three ladies of the party should sit together. She said little to her neighbour, but she ran her eyes to and fro over the men around the table. She knew this kind of company very well, and could foresee the situations that would develop among them—for instance, that old crotchety Oswald the Reeve over there would go out of his way to disagree with almost everyone, especially the clerics; that the Friar and the Pardoner would be at daggers drawn; that the Miller wouldn't care a damn for any of them; that the Skipper would call the poor old Parson a Lollard; and plenty of other personal clashes would arise. Oh, it would be lively enough! And she the only eligible woman among the lot of them—it would be hard if there wasn't *one* potential sweetheart there. . . .

Her eyes, of course, dwelt first on the youngest—the golden-haired Squire, standing by his father's side to carve his meat for him. Her heart would always leap up at a boyish face and a golden head—but too late now. No more of lovely youth for Alison. Past and gone, all those fair days when she could have beautiful boys at her command—yes, and please them better than a virgin in her teens. . . . The wheat's all sold, she said to herself, and now I must sell the chaff as best I can. No matter. . . . Her eyes turned to his father, the Knight. There was a man! Tall, spare, between golden and grey, like a stubble-field after harvest—hard and clean-cut in every line, his blue eyes twinkling with life, a far-away smile on his face as of one who has seen men and cities—that were a man, if perhaps. . . . Or how would that grave-faced Doctor be? No—too gloomy and earnest—too near death's business to be a comfortable companion. See him with his notebook there, writing down the various complaints of which the pilgrims were to pray for healing. Already he had approached Alison before supper and won from her the details of her deafness. Oh no, he'd be a wet-blanket.

Her eyes dwelt for a moment on the Parson, but no one could look at him long with light or impertinent thoughts. There was an air about him that reproved any personal approach, although he radiated loving-kindness and helpfulness. But looking into his eyes was like opening a window on a bright frosty morning—all was sweet, clear, cold, and unearthly. She drew back, awestruck. By his side was the poor Clerk. They made a quiet pair together, with plenty to say to each other but little to those around them; save that when there was need to speak the courtesy of both of them was instant and gracious.

The clerics—the two priests, the Summoner, the

Pardoner, the Monk and the Friar, she could dismiss. A clerical *amour* was always possible, but Alison never fancied it. Perhaps she had never quite forgotten that friar in the woods when she was a girl. . . . There were the five liverymen, but none of them seemed to emerge as a personality. The lawyer? A typical "very busy man,"—no time for dalliance; and anyhow, she knew lawyers. She could recall too plainly poor Watkyn, her second husband; his preoccupied air, his dusty parchments, the dry and serious world he carried with him like a garment—no, *not* the Man of Law. Who else? There was the Franklyn, and she would have liked to observe him more closely—but he was seated just where she could not see him, abreast of her on her deaf side, screened from her by the Prioress. She very much wanted another look at him, for there was something that intrigued her, something that recalled far-away thoughts—if only she could hear his voice clearly! She leant forward, trying to see him on the Prioress's other side.

"Alison," said the Prioress, "I see you've not changed. Still throwing your eyes round at the men. . . ."

"Bitch!" was what Alison wanted to say, but didn't. Only, just as the Prioress, in her niminy-piminy way, was lifting a morsel to her lips, a fine greasy morsel of meat, just dipped in the gravy—with a delicate gesture, and her little finger crooked—Alison jogged her elbow. The morsel fell, moist and messy, on the Prioress's snowy bosom; it rolled down and was snapped up by the lap-dog, but a gross, brown, greasy stain lay all over the fine linen. The Prioress gave a little shriek and cried for her napkin, which her attend-

ant nun obsequiously produced from a bag, with a flask
of rosewater and a pomander. She dabbed ineffectu-
ally at her linen, her face hot with vexation. Then she
turned on Alison.

"You did that on purpose. . . ."

"Not I, dear neighbour," replied Alison. "I thought
you was feeding your dog." The Prioress swallowed
her wrath, with a sip of ale.

At that moment Harry Bailey rapped on the table
with a wooden spoon, and announced his great
story-game.

Each one, he proposed, should tell two stories on
the way to Canterbury, and two on the way back, in
order decided by lot; and the teller of the best story,
by popular vote, should enjoy a dinner at the expense
of the others. The plan was carried with acclamation.

After dinner Alison waited to waylay the host, with
a request. "Let me ride at the left hand of each
story-teller, I beg you, for otherwise I shan't hear a
word as we go along. You know how deaf I am in my
left ear."

"Certainly, madam, nothing easier." He turned to
where another applicant for a favour had appeared—the quiet little man who was said to be the
poet. "And you, sir?"

"Grant me the right hand of the story-teller, please.
Stories are my trade, and I'd like to see if any of them
be worth writing down."

"Why, of course, Master Geoffrey! So—let me
make you acquainted with Mistress Johnson, who will
take the left as you take the right."

The little poet bowed and took her hand solemnly,
and they walked down the hall together. The Prioress,

a few paces off as the crowd began to disperse, observed her. "Ha, she's got a man already," she remarked to the nun.

". . . And what do you think of this game of story-telling, Madame?" the poet asked Alison, by way of making a conversational opening.

"Oh—I'll tell you one thing. They'll never get through that many tales. If anyone's long and overruns his time, they'll not tell more than one each between here and Canterbury, and even then I doubt whether everyone will have a turn; and as for getting back, why, God knows what may befall us all before we take the road home. . . ."

"True, true. Well, if even half of them can tell a good tale each, we shall do well."

When they retired to bed, it was just as Alison had feared. The sleeping accommodation was in a series of attics running the length of the building, with two or three beds in each room; and the women were allotted one room, with two double beds in it. All the dogs came up to bed with them. Alison made haste and got into one of the beds, while the nuns were going through their long and elaborate prayers; she naturally assumed that the two nuns would share the other bed, and it presently became evident that poor ugly Sister Lucy was hoping tremulously for the honour of sharing a bed with her beloved Madam Eglantyne. However, the Prioress, having led her on and enjoyed the emotional situation, announced that she must have the other bed for herself and the dogs. Sister Lucy must sleep with Mistress Johnson.

So the poor nun crept into Alison's bed crying, and went on snivelling for hours while the Prioress disposed herself in state with all her dogs round her on the bed. Sweeting had again given evidence that he was not house-trained.

"I'll not spend another night like this," Alison said to herself.

THREE

Confessio Amantis

MASTER Geoffrey Chaucer settled himself down beside the hearth, and took out his little notebook. The evening was mild and yet clammy—rain had fallen, the air was full of moisture, and the little bit of fire in the big hearth of the inn room was grateful. This was the first night's halt on the road to Canterbury.

Upstairs the sleeping chambers were oppressive and stuffy. Much as the poet loved his fellow-men, he didn't care very much for them at the moment, packed together, snorting and sweating in uneasy sleep under the low rafters . . . it was better down here, with just enough light from the embers to make notes by, and a couple of big blackjacks of wine which he had bespoken earlier. He chose a comfortable spot by the fire, poured himself out a can of wine, and set to thinking.

It had been a good day—a pleasant ride, and an excellent beginning to the story-game. Nearly everyone knew of a good tale, though not all could tell it well. Now, if he could cast them all into verse. . . . There was the Knight's story, a magnificent beginning. He knew the old romances, that fine old fellow, and how to tell them in the traditional way—once upon a time, and all that. Not a new story of course—everyone knew those old romaunts—but it was all in the telling. The dear old chap's own chivalric imagination embroidered it as he went along—one would only need to shape it up. . . . Oh, and then that shocking bawdy story the Miller had told—and then the other, just as bad, that the crusty old Reeve had told to spite the Miller—Lord, Lord! what a rare bit of naught—they'd go finely into verse, and how they would contrast with the Knight's Tale. . . . And how the Lady Prioress had coughed and hemm'd when the Miller began, and had presently wheeled her mule right round and ridden at the back—well, the procession was long enough and those at the back couldn't hear anyway, so she couldn't hear the Reeve's Tale either.

A door creaked and banged to, up above in the gallery that led to the lofts. Chaucer looked up. Alison, her riding mantle cast about her shift, came down the loft stairs almost at a run. Her face was flushed, her hair tossed about—she gasped, bit her lips, her hands worked at her sides; he almost thought she was sobbing.

"Mistress Alison!" he exclaimed. "You look upset—what's the matter?"

"Oh—oh—oh—" She steadied herself against the wing of the settle before she could speak. "Oh, Master Chaucer, I'm—oh, I'm so vexed—I can't bear it, I can't, I declare to God I can't—to be spoken to so—that woman, that creature—I can't sleep in there, I'm stifled—it chokes me—her and her dogs—'' She began crying again.

"Come, come now, pretty lady. Pull yourself together, my dear. Why, you're trembling all over. Sit down and tell an old man all about it. Here, have a cup of wine and you'll feel better.'' He guided her to a seat on the settle, and bit by bit she began to regain control.

"It's that woman up there—Madam Eglantyne, by your leave—Mother, too, save the mark! All she's mother to is those filthy hounds—Now say I called her a bitch! And so she is too—oh, she'll preach at me, will she? She'll hold her head high, and shame me? Just because she's chaste, chaste—because she hasn't got the guts to be anything else—because she's got buttermilk in her veins instead of blood, and couldn't be any good to a man if her life depended on it—she's pure, she's good, she's holy and I, I'm dirt, am I?''

"Why, who says so?'' The mild, elderly blue eyes twinkled a little, but kindly.

"Oh, *she* says so, and she should know. Hasn't she been preaching to me this hour past—no, not *to* me, *at* me—just holding forth on holy chastity, and purity, and virginity—all for the benefit of that poor nun of hers, who's so ill-favoured she couldn't have got a man unless she'd had money, poor lass, but I'll wager she's got hot blood and a fair body, and all she can do is to be lickspittle to her ladyship, who treats her worse than a beast—so the poor lass who has never had the chance to be aught but a virgin gets all this poured out for a side-glance at me. Yes, if you please, Madam Eglantyne's to go straight to a front seat in heaven while poor Alison howls in hell. Alison's to fry

28

in the devil's pan, while *she* sips syllabubs on a cloud featherbed. . . . Why, what do you think—I said to her, 'But didn't our Blessed Saviour Himself go to a wedding?'—and she said to me, 'Only once, the Scripture says—not five times, Alison, not five times!'

She laughed as she told it, but bitterly, and the tears ran down her cheeks.

"Wipe your tears, my dear," said Chaucer. "So she said that, did she? Five times—but what did she mean by that?"

"Didn't you know? Why, it's because I've been married five times, and—"

"Five times, have you?" Chaucer looked at her with interest and respect. "Now, that's something! Five husbands, have you had?"

"Yes, and—and others—"

"Oh, never mind about them! We'll let them be forgotten. But five husbands!"

"Yes, and because of that *she* says I'll burn in hell."

"Why—do you think she's right, then, that you sob so bitterly? Do you repent of them, then?"

"Repent? Why—" She considered, wide-eyed. "Why—no. But oh, I don't know. . . . The things she said . . . Master Chaucer, do you think I'm a very wicked woman?"

"How do I know?" He smiled encouragingly, and filled her can again. "Come, make your confession to me, and I'll see if I can shrive you."

She glanced up at him. "I'd sooner confess to you than to a priest, any day. You're a man—I can talk to you. I don't like women and I don't like priests. All right, I'll tell you my story, and see if you'll give me shrift."

"Make it a comfortable confessional," he said, and

placed a cushion for her in the settle, and another for
himself in the opposite corner. He arranged the two
drinking cans on the seat between them, with the
bottle handy; and so leaned back and let her launch
into her story.

It was an odd story she told him; looking back on it
afterwards, it seemed to her that she must have given
him an impression not quite true to the facts. An impression of herself, for one thing, as a competent
tamer of husbands from the first, bullying and
dominating all five of them as she had bullied poor
Baldwin. The poet had got the five of them mixed up,
too—from questions he asked her, it seemed that he
hadn't bothered much to distinguish one from
another—indeed he had seemed to see them, she
guessed, as five little men grouped all round her at
once, like a Turk's five wives, herself towering over
them. Well, but the poet hadn't listened to all she had
to say—he had led her on about some things, and
skipped over others—her youth and first adventures
he had hardly shown interest in at all, but he led her on
about Baldwin and about Harry too, so that it began to
seem, in the way she told it, as if she had bullied Harry
as she bullied Baldwin. She had her pride to salve
there—yes, and perhaps the pride of Harry's memory
too. It looked better that he should have been nagged
into infidelity by her, and she in turn driven into infidelity by him, than that he should have gone to pieces
in the end in the way he did. And as for Watkyn and
Lucas, they all looked like Baldwin as the story was
told. The poet even got muddled as to the order they
came in—though he got Jenkyn's story clear enough.
The poet seemed to have a fixed picture of her as an

accomplished termagant, with a rolling-pin for any man's head, able to dominate them all. Well, life had made her something like that, but a woman didn't begin that way. Once she had been vulnerable and helpless. . . .

Oh well, the wine was good, and it wasn't as if he was going to put her in a book, like that book of Jenkyn's about Clytemnestra and Hipsi-pipsi-lee.

PART TWO

ALISON'S CONFESSION

ONE

"Other companie in youthe"

IT had all begun on that day in May when Alison had gone out a maid and had come home a maid no more. She said she was twelve, but that was a slight exaggeration. She was thirteen.

Being a maid was a nuisance, but there was something odd and mysterious about being a maid-no-more. When she asked Gamelyn, her favourite brother, about it, he told her evasively to ask their mother; but all the satisfaction that Alison got from her was to emphasize the disadvantages of being a maid.

Alison was the daughter of the miller at Watchet near Bath, and the junior of four brothers. "Mother," she said, "why can't I do what the boys do? Why can't I take service with a shipman and go travelling, like Adam? Or be 'prenticed to a London mercer, like

Tom, or be a clerk at Oxenford like John or even a gamekeeper like Gamelyn?"

"Don't talk nonsense, my maid. Those things be for boys, not for maids."

"I know—but there's no reason for it."

"The Lord has made you a weak woman, my dear—"

"Weak! Why I'm much stronger than John, and I think I'm as strong as Tom and Gamelyn. Tom gives out after he's run five furlongs—I don't. John's so weak I can hold him down with one hand—I've tried! Weak woman indeed!"

"Ah yes, my child, but women just can't do the same things as men. It isn't in nature."

"I don't see why. I want to travel, like Adam—I'll wager I'll travel further some day than ever he will. I want to make money, like the London mercers—I'll do it better than Tom. I could be a clerk like John, I daresay—"

"Thee a clerk! Child, you don't even pay attention when you go to the classes at the convent. Edith, now—"

"Oh, beshrew Edith, and the convent classes! I can learn nothing from those old beldame nuns. They know nothing themselves, anyway. They're not clerks. Oh, Mother, isn't there anything a girl is allowed to do?"

"Why, my dear, she must marry and be a wife and a mother—that is her lot and her bliss, and the Lord approves it."

"Oh, that's not what I want—that's just to belong to a man and ask him for everything. I want to do things, and be somewhat, and go about the world—"

"My dear," said her mother, looking very wise,

"marry the right man and you'll have all you desire."

"I tell you, mother, I don't want to be married."

"Tut, my child—listen now. There's one in view for you already—a good husband if ever there was one, if you've the sense to know it—"

Sudden warm romantic suggestions, like flower perfumes in summer, wafted across to her. Some tall, noble, ardent young man, as the stories told—who might he be? Marriage might even be bearable, if love were indeed such a rich pleasure as the stories said—

"Oh, mother, who?"

The next words were a frost over the flowers.

"Master Lucas the corn-merchant."

"Oh, but mother—he's old! he's old!"

"Fifty-nine—well, a little more—none so bad, my child."

"Nigh as old as father."

"He'll treat you fatherly—and he'll trouble you the less with childbearing. My dear, he's a rich man and a good man and a kind man—be patient with him and he'll give you all your heart can desire."

(But *all* my heart can desire? she thought. Not all that a young, ardent, gallant sweetheart could give.)

"His head's bald—his teeth are bad—his chaps are fallen in—he has hairs growing out of his nose—"

"For all that, he's a very worthy gentleman, and a good match for you."

An uneasy silence fell between them.

"Unless, my dear love," said her mother, "you'd consider the life of religion? I should like to see you a blessed holy sister, especially as none of the boys will choose to be priests."

"Me a holy sister? Not likely!" said Alison with alacrity.

"Farmer Ditton's Edith, now—she's to take the veil as soon as she is old enough, and what a joy that will be to her dear parents!"

"A joy to everybody, to get her out of the way," said Alison. "Farmer Ditton's Edith is a fish-blooded, whey-faced ninny. The convent's welcome to her, but I—oh, mother, do I look like a nun?"

She stood, the firelight glowing back from her glowing cheeks—a buoyant, rounded, intensely living figure; the rosy flesh triumphing in every line. Her mother smiled as she sighed.

"Well no, my dear, I'm afraid you don't."

And at that moment, of course, Friar John must needs come in.

Dame Prout liked Friar John very much; Alison didn't like him at all. He was round and unctuous with soft, red, flabby lips and cheeks that were pink and white like a baby's; he had a honeyed tenor voice, and he made himself very much at home wherever he went. He was a "limitor," that is, a begging Franciscan licensed by the Bishop to beg in a certain district, which he might not go beyond. Friar John did very well in his district, and at the mill in particular—when Miller Prout was out of the way. Miller Prout didn't like Friar John any more than Alison did—but there, one of the things little Alison had begun to notice was that it was no use father making a fuss about anything, if mother really wanted it so. Alison had no idea how it was done—as yet; but she knew that her father dare not say a word against Friar John, though he might grit his teeth when he saw the big monk's figure go past the wheelhouse door towards the kitchen—and mutter, and shuffle his feet as if he longed to take a running kick at that broad, brown backside. . . .

But Friar John had the run of the place; in he would come and take possession of the kitchen; turn out Gib the cat from his corner in the settle, which of course was the only corner free from draughts, and establish his lordly person there—spreading his legs out, turning up the skirt of his habit over his knees to warm his feet at the fire.

"*Benedicite*, my children," he would chant in his honey-sweet voice. "The dear Lord save you, good mistress! Have you a crust of bread for a poor brother today?"

Crust of bread, the old humbug! Out would come the best in the house—a strong ale in a latten tankard, fine white manchet bread, and a dozen or so new-laid eggs, a dish of cream, fresh butter, junkets and syllabubs and marchpane, and soft sweet pears off the wall. Nothing was too good for the Friar. And there he would sit, laying down the law to all the house.

"In good time, Friar John," said Dame Prout. "I was bewailing that my Alison here won't think of taking the holy vows."

"No? Is that so?" And the Friar ran his eye up and down her. "Pity. She'd have made a sweet little nun, would you not, baggage?—Come here, child—I won't hurt you. How she grows! Not fourteen yet, you say—and here's a bosom a princess might envy. Let alone, child, I do but admire thee as thy father in God. Let's see—are thine arms as thin as they were? By cock, they've grown plumper. . . ."

"Leave go of me, you lewd old man!" exclaimed Alison, pulling herself away from him.

"Why Alison, there's a way to speak to the good Friar," her mother scolded her. "You should be ashamed. Beg his pardon at once."

"I won't beg his pardon. It's he that should be ashamed," she maintained, looking them both stoutly in the face.

"Nay, then, mistress, you shall be whipped," said Dame Prout.

"Oh, let me do the whipping, good dame!" insinuated the Friar. "I'd chastise her so lovingly—yes I would—I'd melt her hard heart—oh pray you, let me try—"

But Alison thought this the best moment to make a quick getaway.

And so she came to that May morning. Oh, the glory of those May mornings! After the smoky, dark, painful winter, with its miserable poor feeding, its weariness, its sicknesses, the isolation from the world, the struggle to keep alive . . . the translation to summer was as from hell to heaven. The unbelievable exaltation—the strange, living light casting crisp shadows under apple-trees and beech-trees—the mist, a tender grey-purple bloom staining the blue sky for "the pride of the morning"—the dew, heavy on southernwood and rosemary—the scents, and the bird-song, and the sudden warmth—

There might be useful work to be done around the mill and its kitchen—but for Alison the important thing was to get out into it and as far away from home as possible. Without a by-your-leave or with-your-leave, off she went over meadows and stiles for the gay greenwood—early, before the sun was high, before anyone might notice her. The first of May, and who wouldn't go a-maying?

Where she crossed the stile into the next lane she met Farmer Ditton's Edith, demure and tidy—her face scrubbed and her hair scraped back. She was on her way to the convent, carrying a rosary.

"Why, Alison! Aren't you coming to Mass?"

"Not me," said Alison. "I'm going a-Maying. What a day to go to Mass!"

"Why, but it's the Feast of Philip and James—"

"Philip and James!" In forceful terms, Alison indicated where the holy Apostles might go, what they might do, and also what they might be. Edith winced.

"Oh, Alison, you wicked girl! How dare you say such things! If the Reverend Mother heard you, she'd give you penance."

"And that would be nothing new. Seems to me I do penance every Sunday for one thing or another. I'll not do penance for holy Philip and James as well."

"No, but Alison, think! If Sister Clemency heard you!" Edith's voice was sugary with reverential sentiment.

"Oh, Sister Clemency!" mocked Alison. "Edith, I do believe if you were a boy you'd be in love with her!"

Edith winced again. "Alison, you do say dreadful things. You ought to be ashamed of yourself. Sister Clemency is so good, and so beautiful, and so sweet and saintly and wonderful—and she's never going to let any horrid man touch her, but she's always going to remain a pure virgin, like Saint Cecilia—I'm sure Saint Cecilia wasn't half so lovely." The girl was stock-still in the middle of the lane, dreaming, her eyes on a spray of wild cherry. Alison lolled against the stile, displaying her shapely brown legs carelessly. Edith, warmed by her own eloquence and wanting a listener, came over towards her and sat down primly and carefully on the stile, smoothing her dress down. "Nay, you may mock, Alison, but let me tell you. Father has consented that I should enter Saint Winifred's as a postulant as soon as I'm sixteen. Won't that be wonderful? To live in a beautiful convent, and have everything quiet and genteel, and do embroidery, and sing, and speak French—no rough horrid men and boys to disturb you—never have to get married and have a lot of nasty babies . . . I'd have a lot of dogs instead, like they do at Saint Winifred's, and cats and white pigeons, and a white mule. . . . I'd have a beautiful blue-edged veil like Sister Clemency. . . . Don't you think it ould be lovely?"

"Pah!" said Alison. "Not for me. You have it if you want it. But none of your convents for me. Each man to his liking, but . . ." Words failed her, so she got down rather abruptly off the stile. "Well, God b'with 'ee. I'll go pick bluebells. Give my love to holy Philip and James."

She was off over the fields, while Edith, after sighing and casting hands and eyes up to heaven, in imitation of Sister Clemency, went on her way to the convent.

Alison climbed the bank into my Lord Hatherleigh's covert, and went through the bluebell wood, and on and on. Here all was sheer enchantment; March and April had been yellow and green, but here blue and white were added, with sometimes the blush of a flowering crab-apple, and the first dog-rose. Sunshine soaked through the thin fresh leaves like honey into the honeycomb; and everywhere was music of birds, and the little sounds of life.

She remembered one night when she had gone poaching with Gamelyn and had seen, or dreamt she saw, little silver dancers on the moss, moving in a ring. . . . But that was the first and last time she had gone out at night with Gamelyn, such an uproar there had been at home when her adventure was discovered. So she had never been able to look for the little people again. Perhaps she would see them again today, if she went far enough into the wood. Surely this was the day of all days to see them, when blossom and leaf rioted in glory, and the air was all fragrance?

So she went on and on, deep into glade after glade, each more enchanting than the last. Out of the paths she knew and far beyond—she had never been so far before. Up beech slopes, down into dells filled with bluebells, through spongy damp brakes of silver birches, into the clear again, more beeches and more bluebells—

And then a check, for as she parted a covert and entered a new glade, there was a brown friar walking up and down in the sunshine.

Not their own Friar John, but a strange limitor from some other boundary—a big, rough, hairy fellow. He was pacing to and fro in the glade, getting the sunshine—he might have been saying his prayers, but Alison thought not; he had his frock thrown open and tucked back under either arm, and was exposing himself to the sunlight in a manner far from discreet.

When he saw her he rounded his eyes, and pursed his thick moist lips to a whistle—then opened them to let out a hunter's yell, and leapt towards poor little Alison with arms outstretched.

She was rooted to the spot with panic for a moment—then she fled.

Panic terror beyond all description possessed her; every kind and degree and element of fear—plain animal instinct of flight, shocked repugnance at the obscenity and foulness of the thing that followed her; creepy, almost superstitious dread, and fear of the unknown . . . all these, and worse. If it had been some bloodthirsty beast that would kill and devour her and be done with it, she would have been less terrified. Added to this, the sheer physical anguish of bursting lungs, labouring heart, rasping throat, flagging legs. . . .

Pray? She prayed to the Blessed Virgin, but no thunderbolt fell—only the awful thing came on. Dodge from the path like a rabbit? She might get cornered, and anyhow had hardly the wit left to contrive it. Turn and fight—as many a time she had kicked and bitten her brothers?—No, she couldn't . . . never in her life had she felt so undefended, her flesh so soft and vulnerable. Plead with her pursuer, as a man, to spare her? But this was neither a man nor an animal, but something far worse.

He was gaining on her, gaining on her—then her strength gave out, she tripped and fell, and the friar, laughing madly and obscenely, leapt upon her where she lay. She gave a long, despairing shriek and felt the brute starting to tear at her clothes. But in that moment, and before he could attain his purpose, suddenly a shout—a young voice, fresh but strangely deep, crying, "What's this? You friar, what are you about?"—and then her persecutor started back off her and was suddenly gone. She sat up—the friar was running down the path up which she had just run—a tall young man was whirling a cudgel behind him—a long leg shot out and sped the friar on his way from behind—and then as the range increased, a shower of handy flints, and some very choice abuse.

"Get out of it, you nasty old lecher—I'll teach you to ravish maidens. If you turn round one step, I'll cut your itching flesh off your scabby bones. God's blood, are we to have the country defiled with old ramping goats like thee? Get back to your cloister if you've got one. . . ." A lucky hit with a flint cut the shaven crown, and drew blood. "Aha, that lets some of your hot blood out. By the Mass, I'll cool off the lot of it if you ever show your misbegotten face here—" And much more that could hardly be set down. And having seen that friar safely out of sight, the rescuer turned back to Alison.

She was leaning back against the trunk of a tree, rather feebly trying to put herself to rights—and even in dishevelment she was rather charming, reminding him, with her tawny hair and big greenish eyes, of a ginger kitten that had been chased by the dogs and now, in a safe spot, was trying to lick its fur into order.

Alison was completely dead-beat and for several minutes could do no more than lie against the tree, as limp as a rag doll, struggling with her breath, waiting for her heart to stop pumping. She shut her eyes, for everything had gone dark and red for a moment; then she felt she was going to be sick; but when she opened her eyes she changed her mind. The young man standing over her was a heartening enough sight to bring her back to equilibrium. Indeed he was good to look upon, being very tall and broad-shouldered, about twenty perhaps, beardless but with a little golden down on his lip, his hair golden too, and golden hairs on his arms and his neck. He had well-shaped features and uncommonly pleasant grey eyes, which were regarding Alison with flattering concern. From his dress he might be a yeoman's son or a young farmer.

"It's all right," he was saying, "he's gone, that brute. He won't come back. He'd better not! Did he hurt you, sweetheart?"

"No." She began to explore herself for bruises—she had a few, and her plump elbow and one side of her face were grazed where she had measured her length on the ground.

"Oh, but your poor pretty cheek—and your arm—what a shame. They're all rubbed on the ground."

His voice was peculiarly deep-pitched—soft and vibrant, and very pleasant. She began to dab at her cheek and elbow with her apron. He took a corner of the apron and tenderly wiped her face.

"Did he—do anything to you? What he was trying to do, I mean?"

"No—oh no." She felt faint again at the memory of her panic. "But oh, I was so frightened."

"I know. You're shaking still. Don't think about it anymore. What can we do?—ah, I know."

He had a leather bottle at his belt, full of strong dry wine; he made her drink some of it, straight from the bottle. It did her good, and presently he found her a more comfortable resting-place, a nest of beech-leaves, deep under overhanging boughs. He sat beside her, soothing and comforting her, and it seemed only to be expected that his arms should be round her, as if she were a child that he was protecting. She liked him—she decided in her mind that touching him, and being touched by him, was good and pleasant; and she relaxed by his side.

"Won't you tell me your name, sweetheart?"

"I'm Alison—Miller Prout's Alison of Watchet Mill. And you?"

"My name's Gilbert."

"Gib! That's my cat's name. You're rather like him—you've a purring voice, and you're tawny-orange colour, as he is."

He laughed. "Do you love Gib your cat, then?"

"Oh yes—he sleeps with me—"

"Do you wish I was he?"

"Oh you're too big—and naughty." She giggled, and then suddenly turned pale and shuddered again.

"What is it, love?"

"That man—that horrible friar. Oh—he frightened me so. I shall be frightened of all men now. Frightened of having a man touch me, like Edith is." (And yet she didn't move away from him.) "Shall I have to go into a convent, like Edith? I couldn't bear the thought of getting married now."

He considered her gravely.

"That isn't good. A girl shouldn't be afraid of love. Don't go into a convent, little Alison. You'll forget your fright."

"Oh, I don't think I could—ever—"

"No, no, my dear. That old brute was enough to frighten any maid, but some day, please God, when the right man comes along—one quite young, like yourself, and perhaps good-looking too—"

"Hah." She grinned at him. "You're talking like a grandfather. You're not so old yourself—and you're good-looking too—"

She turned towards him, and looked long and deep into his grey eyes.

"Now if it were you—it would be different—"

He nodded gravely. "It would be different. . . ."

Later, Alison lay looking up dreamily through oceans and oceans of beech-leaves to the blue sky. Gilbert, in the exhausted aftermath of passion, lay with his head between her breasts; mechanically she caressed his crisp tawny hair.

So this was it—that thing they all talked about with such fear and delight and mystery. Yes, it was a princely pleasure—a pleasure worth giving wealth and worldly honours for. Worth one's immortal soul? She wondered. . . . But did the priests really know? And what about that friar, if it came to that?—Still, she didn't seem to feel any difference in her immortal soul, as far as she could tell—except that she had suddenly grown very fond of this dear, tall, passionate, gentle boy, whose face she had seen break into such a smile of complete beatitude and who now lay so helpless between her breasts.

Everything was sunny and sweet and quiet—so quiet. As quiet as God's first Saturday, and as good.

Late that afternoon as the sun began to decline, she tripped homeward very happily, singing a little song to herself and glowing with a quiet, new-found rapture. But as she got within reach of her home, she began to run till she was sufficiently out of breath; then she stopped and disordered her hair, put grit from the road on her face and arms, and even tore her dress at the neck—and so, running again, reached the mill and staggered into her mother's arms.

"Oh mother, mother, I'm ravished! The friar in the wood—oh, mother, mother, I'm a maid no more!"

She found herself an object of solicitude and commiseration—fussed over, pitied, exclaimed over as the innocent victim and not scolded at all. So far, so good.

Her father swore horribly. "If it's that Father John—God's blood and bones, I'll geld him."

"Oh no, no, no," she hastened to assure him. "It wasn't Friar John. It was a strange limitor, one I'd never seen before—it was a long way off, belike in the next parish."

"The Archdeacon should be told of it," growled her father. "Anyhow, I don't trust one of them. Wife, I'm not having that Father John in the place anymore."

Alison's mother, standing defiantly behind the chair into which Alison had collapsed, retorted, "You heard her say it wasn't Father John. What had he to do with it then? If he'd been there he'd have seen she came to no harm. Poor lamb, and thee all alone out of call of help! How could thee resist the friar, then?"

"Mother—is it a very, very terrible sin?"

"Why, my love, that's for the priest to say. But Father John shall absolve thee."

"He'd better," growled the miller.

So, amid sympathy and tender concern, the poor ravished victim was led off to bed.

—And lay there smiling. So far, so very good. All was excused and forgiven—she'd be safe in this world and presumably the next. And tomorrow at noon she was to meet Gilbert again. He was to tell her then when, where, and by what means he could marry her.

And she would lie in his arms once more, and hold that dear tawny head on her breast, and hear his deep, soft, purring voice. She laughed as she clasped Gib-Cat to her, and fondled him as she fell asleep.

Anya Seton

And she would lie in his arms once more, and hold that dear tawny head on her breast, and hear his deep, purring voice. She...ached as she...clasped...the Ca......her...nestled......e shorteli......

TWO
First Husband

ONLY the thick curtains separated Alison, in her truckle-bed, from her parents. In the grey of dawn their voices woke her.

"Wife—suppose our Alison were to prove with child?"

"Oh, but that wouldn't happen—a holy friar—"

"God's patience, is there no end to the silliness of women? A holy friar's a man, isn't he? And more of a man than some, too—and a girl can conceive by him, I warrant."

"Why—one never hears of a girl got with child by a friar, and everyone knows that they—"

"Is that so? Then Father John had best keep out of this house, the pest rot his guts! But if you want to know why you never hear of a friar's child, it's because they marry the girl off quick—and that's what we must do with Alison."

Alison, listening, froze in her bed.

"Maybe you're right, Will."

"I'll say I am. Tomorrow I'll speak to Master Lucas, and we'll have them haltered up before the month's out—before there's signs of trouble, whether or not. Better be sure than sorry."

So Alison lay and heard sentence passed on her. She did not cry—the panic and anxiety were too great for that. Only she lay clenching her fists and biting her lips, waiting, waiting for the morning to come, that she might fly to the tryst and tell Gilbert he must save her.

When at last the rest of the household stirred, and she might rise also and open the wooden shutters that closed the unglazed windows, a grey sky met her, and a steady downpour of rain. But surely the rain wouldn't stop him? All the morning she fidgeted about the mill, fussing round the calves in the byre so as to have a good reason to put on her wooden pattens and her thick woollen cloak. At last, when from the priory bell she judged it to be about an hour before noon, she slipped away, through the unceasing rain, down the flooded lanes, into the soaking, dripping wood. All the time she never doubted he would be there.

They had marked a spot, a great beech-tree at the intersection of two paths, where they should meet. They couldn't miss. As she got near she began to think how she looked—to smooth back her hair and try to set her bodice in order, and wipe the raindrops from her face; but who could look pretty in that rain? She came in sight of the trysting spot. No one there. No matter, he would come soon.

So she waited. Oh, he would come soon, surely he would come soon. . . .

Surely he would come, surely. . . . Surely. . . .

Hope died very hard as she stood there wet and cold and weary in the falling rain. She reasoned with herself, she made excuses for him, she gave him a little longer—and a little longer still.

At last, when the watery light behind the clouds that had not lifted all day began to fall westward, she knew it was useless. She gave one deep sob, let the hood fall over her face, and turned for home—beaten. There she slipped in and up to her bed, and lying there, wept. Her mother, hearing her, said, "Poor child, poor child—" and thought she was weeping for her betrayal. Which, indeed, she was.

So little Alison was married, almost before she knew it, and became Mistress Lucas, merchant's wife and sad matron, before she was two months older.

The wedding took place in July and was held in Bath, where Master Lucas, a rich man these twenty years past, had a fine town house in the new style—all carving and crotchets without, all panel and polish within. For Alison's marriage was a step up in the world.

The family went over from Watchet on pack-horses and mule-carts and ox-carts, an awful cumbersome procession, with her dowry and dresses and linen—including some sheets and blankets she had spun and woven herself. Not as many as an older bride might have had, but done even then with skill and finish, for Alison had quite early shown a considerable aptitude for spinning and weaving.

It was a fine, noisy, convivial wedding with lots to eat and drink laid out on trestles in Master Lucas's garden. Alison felt sick halfway through the feast, and had to vanish hastily—her mother carefully concealing the fact, for though it would be quite in order for the new-made wife to be queasy *after* the wedding-night, it would not be so fitting before. . . .

Then came all the traditional business of putting the bridal couple to bed. The undressing of the bride was made much of, and a crowd of kinswomen and play-fellows buzzed around Alison like bees around their queen, with laughter and tittering and bold mock-modesty and honeyed sentiment—for all the world as if it were some handsome young sweetheart she were marrying. Down the corridor, the menfolk were undressing the bridegroom too, with loud laughter and plenty to drink, and broad hearty jokes about virginity and virility and fecundity and cuck-oldry. Alison could hear her father's voice, and knew he was well lit up—Master Lucas was the same, and he and Miller Prout seemed to be singing in chorus and swearing eternal fellowship. Her brothers Adam, Tom, and Gamelyn were there too—Adam trying to keep her father within bounds, Gamelyn a bit sub-dued, for that he knew he was losing his dear compan-ion. As for John, he had disappeared with one of the bridesmaids as soon as the feast had ended, and would probably be occupying a comfortable corner of the stable with her. Men could do as they pleased. . . .

Then they put her into bed and made her all fine and pretty, and led in Master Lucas, smirking and stagger-ing, in a fine brocaded nightgown and a tasselled night-cap, and helped him into bed beside her. Alison lay tense and tight and motionless.

Her mother, as was customary, drew the curtains on the happy pair, and gave them her blessing; and the whole company sang a crude little rhyme outside the door and left them.

Alison, shutting her eyes tight, wondered if she could pretend to herself that this was Gilbert.

But in a very few minutes she knew that she could not. . . . She knew only too well that this was nothing like Gilbert, nor ever could be; and she knew too that she would have to exert all the flattery, all the arts her inexperience could think of, to make it credible to Master Lucas that this was his child that she carried.

And the next day she had to put on a heavy, sad-coloured stuff gown, down to her feet, and a cap over her tawny hair, and take the housekeeper's keys at her girdle—keys which Master Lucas's two daughters by his first wife, already soured virgins at twenty-five, would never allow her to use with any authority. From now onward, her body growing heavier every day even without the weight of the thick gown, she had to learn to tend her old husband, watch his wealth and not spend it, and submit herself to her stepdaughters. And on a cold morning in February, she, no more than a child herself, gave birth to a child whom she called Gilbert—nobody ever knowing why she chose that name.

THREE
Second Husband

SLOWLY and with much consequence, the black-clothed procession came across the fields, the bell tolling as they went. And Alison was now a widow.

Three years had gone by, three years that were like a dark tunnel of heaviness and oppression, child-rearing, sick-tending—the long nights when first Gilbert cried, and then Lucas woke and grumbled, and had to be coaxed to sleep, and no sleep for Alison till the dawn was grey, and the day to be faced—years when she felt she was old, old and tired—listening of an evening to the gay young people going by in the street, dancing and singing "carols"—round-games where they chose partners, danced, and kissed. And when the spring came round, the soft dusk and the scent of the trees tore at her heart. She would weep quietly, when she could get time alone, for her lost lover, but more for her lost youth; but she was so seldom left alone. Lucas, impotently affectionate, would have her always by his side, doting, caressing—sickening her. But besides him there were Elizabeth and Catherine jealously on the watch, taking no trouble to conceal their hatred of her, their suspicion of her pretty face, their sour old-maidish dislike of poor baby Gilbert. They spread their thick dark skirts and sat round her like a besieging army. "Why do they watch me?" she used to ask herself. "What do they think I'll do—'ods pittikins, steal the old man's money, or let another man in by the back door?" If, in those disturbing days of April and May, sobs rose in her throat and tears in her eyes, it was, "How now, sulky? What's the matter with thee? Did your mother teach you no manners, then—or do they always sulk with the damp in a millhouse?" And if she cried in bed there was Lucas, with his sickening offers of consolation. Finally she had to take to going to church often, so as to have a good cry there. And even there the sisters would follow her, and see her in tears, and make scathing remarks about vain contrition for faults that were never mended.

She was shut off, too, from her kindred—Bath was a good way from Watchet, over such roads as there were—as much as fifteen miles were enough to put a lifelong gap between friend and friend, especially in the winter. Besides, the Lucas sisters did not encourage the Prout family. The miller and his trade were low, the house was rude, the folk there lived like pigs—and they told Alison so, very often. All those three years they let her see her mother once only, at Gilbert's christening. Her father and Master Lucas remained firm friends, but Catherine and Elizabeth did their best to freeze the miller out when he came to see them. The boys were away on their various trades.

One other friend Alison had, or might have had—that was her godmother Alison Barton. She was a cheerful, sensible woman, the wife of a smallholder, living some miles out of Bath; a great influence in Alison's childhood, and always helpful. Alison might have appealed to her when her trouble first arose, but it so happened that godsib Alison was at that time lying sick of a fever, and when she was well again, all had been settled, and it was useless for the kindly godmother to protest to the family about the unsuitability of the match. Godsib Alison had a forthright tongue, and had said what she thought about Elizabeth and Catherine; therefore it wasn't surprising that they called her a freespoken housewife, and forbade her their doors. So Alison was alone. She had baby Gilbert to love, but he tried her patience sorely—she was only fifteen and not very maternal by nature; and you couldn't talk much to a baby.

As to the dignity and authority of a married woman—where was that? She was kept more in subjection than ever she had been in her childhood—she was treated as more of a child now, but no longer young. She had no privilege of any kind, neither of youth nor age—she was a slave, an underling, a machine that tended her baby, and made her old husband's posset, and went to bed, and submitted to his clammy hands, and slept little, and woke to begin again. . . .

And now he was gone. Now a sudden seizure had at last palsied him, and after three months another stroke had carried him off, and they had just laid him in the churchyard with all the pomp that money could buy.

Alison, veiled in black from head to foot, walked demurely, leaning on Catherine's most unsympathetic arm. Elizabeth came behind, with some aged kinsmen gathered for the occasion. A number of friends followed, for Master Lucas had been well respected too, for all that it would not induce any man to court his daughters. . . . The long, black, wavering line came along between the fields. Back at the house there would be wine and cakes, served first to the men by the womenfolk waiting on them in silence; when the men had finished and withdrawn, the women would eat and drink alone. And then the family would gather, and the will would be read.

And Alison thought, "Now I'm free, I'm free. I've done with him. I'm not his wife anymore, not anyone's wife. Perhaps I shall be able to get back to father and mother. Oh, shall I be able to fling off these coifs and skirts, and let my hair down, and be young again? I'm still only seventeen."

They reached the door, and various people greeted her. There flashed into her mind Master Watkyn, the lawyer in his dangling black hood, and with the sight of him came the thought—money. Now as a widow she'd have money of her own. Not to have to ask the old man for every groat, but have money to spend herself. . . .

Master Watkyn bowed very low over her hand, pressing it. There was surprising warmth and moisture in such an old hand. And beside him came his young clerk—and he, too, pressed Alison's hand and bowed over it. And her pulses stirred, ever such a little. There were still men in the world, young, fresh, fine, charming men. . . .

The formality of the feast was over, even to the

women's part of it; the guests had withdrawn, all save the lawyer and his clerk; and seated in the panelled soler around the fire, the business of reading the will was begun.

It was an autumn day, sunny and serene and brisk; a good day for new beginnings. Everything looked good in the still clear sunshine; the big bunch of rosemary in a brass pot in the grate, the black hangings that draped the chimney-piece over it, and partly hid the tapestries round the walls (how Alison's mother had exclaimed with pride at them when she came over to see Gilbert's christening!)—the polished latten mugs and plates on the dresser—the rich black dresses of the sisters, with their velvet and jet beads—everything looked opulent, polished, and impressive. Old Watkyn seated himself at the head of the table, setting down his emptied glass with a gesture of satisfaction; Elizabeth and Catherine took their places each side of him, rustling their skirts as they sat, and slightly rattling their jet beads; and Alison took the foot of the table, stepping into her place with dignity and feeling herself already the heiress. The clerk stood behind old Watkyn, deferentially, and more than once his bold, warm, black eyes encountered Alison's, and left her wondering. . . .

Watkyn spread out the stiff parchment rolls and began reading. It was a long, cumbersome business, and as much of it was in queer French and equally queer Latin, nobody but Watkyn and the clerk made any pretence of understanding it at all. The English part, when they came to it, was all "whereases" and "heretofores"—but gradually the sense emerged. And as it did so, Alison, who had been tense with eagerness, found herself hot and cold with rage, disappointment, and frustration.

Master Lucas's considerable fortune was left for the most part in equal moiety to his dear daughters Elizabeth and Catherine. A small livelihood was left in trust for his son Gilbert, under the administration of his godparents.

"And I devise and bequeath to my dearly loved second wife Alison, the sum of Twenty Pounds a year, with her board and keep, for so long as she marry not, but live chaste and honest as becomes a widow; and for that she is yet full young, I direct that this my bequest to her be at the control and dispence of my daughters aforementioned, commending her to their care and guidance, she to be obedient and buxome to them, and they in all things to be her entire governesses, until she come to the age of twenty-five years."

Alison's cheeks reddened, and her heart pounded so that she longed to undo her tight black bodice. The mean old lozel! Oh, the scurvy, cheese-paring, creeping, money-grubbing, bird-liming old Judas . . . twenty pounds indeed . . . and they to be her entire governesses . . . for that she is yet full young. . . . Oh, the foul, shabby, scabby old spawn of Satan—Her mind threw up a fountain of abusive words, which she had no means to let loose. She dared not even frown very much; she had learnt in those past years not to show any feelings in front of her tyrants. So now she sat, red-faced and hot, digging her nails into the palms of her hands. So she had but changed her bondage for a worse one, and that old bag of itching bones, whom she had spent three years humouring and cossetting and flattering, had betrayed her from his grave. Oh, God, and what was her life now going to be?

The reading ended: Watkyn stood up, politely

declined another cup of malmsey, bowed to all three ladies and prepared to go. This time he greeted the sisters first, and bowed very low over their hands, as in duty bound to the heiresses, and left Alison to the last; but as he bent over her hand, he lingered, and held it, and looked up at her pretty round face (and her blazing anger had made her look very charming)—and she began to wonder—what the devil, old fellow? And as for the clerk—but old Watkyn nudged and beckoned him on in a hurry.

"And so now, Alison," said Elizabeth, "I think it best that you should move out of the front chamber tomorrow and let me have it. Catherine will take my room; and you and the child can have the room over the gate."

It's come, then, thought Alison.

"And Alison," said Catherine, "you had better let me keep that gold chain for you. You'll need no gauds while you're in mourning, and you might lose it meantime. It will be safer with me."

"And you'll keep that chance-begotten brat of yours out of our sight, and quieter," pursued Elizabeth.

Alison wheeled about, her back to the wall.

"What's that you say?"

"You heard me. We know well enough he's none of our poor father's. He might be a fool, God rest his soul, but we're not. Bastard I should have said, and bastard I'll say. For the sake of the family's good name we've said nothing up to now, nor will we; but we know for all that, baggage, and you'd best mind your ways, and keep your base come-by-chance under governance. I mean it, and you know me."

Not one word could Alison utter, between rage and fear. Her legs shook under her, but she managed to curtsey to Elizabeth, and staggered out past her, white-faced now and biting her lips. As, curiously weak, she pulled herself step by step up the fine wooden staircase, the window at the turn showed her the street again, and old Watkyn, after maybe another visit to a neighbour, getting on his fat easy pony—yes, and dawdling over it, looking up at the window.

". . . So long as she marry not, but live chaste and honest as becomes a widow. . . ." So long as she marry not! So she was to be tied to those bitches, for the sake of a measly twenty pounds a year which she would never touch—oh, to hell with his twenty paltry pounds!

The sun of a fresh, light-heavened morning was rising, and somewhere a rooster crowed; there were snowdrops in the gardens, and there would be more in the woods—Valentine's Day was come, and the rooks in the high trees were loud with delight. Alison, a grey mantle over her head and clogs on her feet, stole out of the back door of Master Lucas's town house, now for six months past known as Mistress Lucas's house, but not as hers. Mistress Elizabeth ruled there now.

Alison had asked Dorothy, the maid, to look after Gilbert for the day and see he had his food—she wanted a present to give the girl, but had hardly anything of her own to give her; so she gave her a lace handkerchief she had picked up when one of the sisters had dropped it. This was stealing, she knew, but she was desperate. Her only other possession, the gold chain Lucas had given her, and which she had thieved out of Catherine's coffer, she now wore under her dress, keeping it for another purpose.

She slipped round the little quiet streets, and waited

at the corner, till Tod the carter came along. Tod drove his slow, lumbering cart once a week round the villages outside Bath, carrying parcels for the neighbourhood, taking the full six days for some twenty miles circuit, stopping at every inn, sleeping at certain ones and getting drunk at others. Two hours' ride in his lumbering contraption would bring her, in much less time than she could walk, to her godsib Alison Barton's—it was she above all others that she longed to see.

The cart rolled up—a big, cumbersome wagon, with iron-tyred wheels like a farm-cart, and a barrel-shaped hood; it took three big horses, harnessed tandem-wise, to draw it.

"Can thee take me to Spinners Hill?"

"Oh ay, Spinners Hill—but hast thou money to pay, lass?"

"Yes, I've money—or as good," she said, faltering a little.

"All right—get in then. You'll find company aboard. Hey—you Butterbox—haul up lady—dame—*verstand ye?*"

A tousled, blond head appeared from the back curtains of the wagon, two round, marble-like blue eyes, and a friendly grin; a big paw was outstretched, and a cheerful young foreign voice said, "*Kom op, ja?*" and Alison found herself lifted into the wagon. As it jolted slowly off she took stock of her fellow-passenger.

He was a big sprawling fair youth, about her own age, with something odd and outlandish about his dress, and his general shape, and his way of staring at her, with his mouth open as if he wanted to say something but hadn't quite the words. She couldn't quite size him up by the details of his costume, but close to his feet was something she knew all about—a loom, far better than her mother's, larger too, partly wrapped round with sacking for transport; and he was sitting on bales of spun yarn, prepared for the weaver.

He greeted her in funny halting English, and made her a seat on the bales.

"Oh, a loom!" she exclaimed. "Are you a weaver?"

"Ja, mistress, weaver. From Ghant," he smiled at her.

"Gaunt? Where's that? I've heard of John O' Gaunt."

"No, no," he laughed, shaking his head, and pointing his finger at himself. "Not John of Ghant. Pieter of Ghant. Pieter. You?"

"Alison—" she checked herself, and was going to say "Mistress Lucas," and then thought that it might be discreeter not to.

"Elsa. So we call it. Ja, I am a weaver. From Ghant in Nederlands—de Low Countries."

"Oh, a Hollander. I have you. You're a foreigner?" She stared at him with interest—she had never seen a foreigner before, save for an occasional Welshman. "Why are you here, then?"

"Oh, I come because of the church." She looked puzzled. "For the religion. My people, they do not like the church over there."

"I don't like the church much myself," said Alison frankly. "The catechisms and preachings are so dull, and the prayers so long, and I don't like friars and priests and convents. Only they think you awfully wicked if you say so."

"So—yes. Even because so, my father and mother

65

they run away. The priests say they are heretics."

A light began to dawn on Alison.

"Oo—you don't mean to say you're a Lollard?"

"A Lollard? I do not know that name. What is that?"

"Well, it's a—it's a—oh, I don't know, but if you are one you'll have to keep it awfully quiet. They say it's a dreadful thing to be. You'd better not tell anyone, if you are."

The cart jolted, and in her excitement she almost slid off the bale of yarn—he put his arm round her to steady her.

"Then you will not tell anyone of me?"

"Me? No, of course I won't tell. I like you and I think you're a good fellow—and if Lollards are bad men, why I just don't believe you are one, that's all."

"Danks, mevrouw," he said very solemnly, and held her just a little more tightly. She had a feeling that the conversation was getting a trifle personal. "Tell me about your weaving," she said.

"Oh ja—I weave cloth. I take this loom here to the good wife Jackson at Overbrook, and I stay to teach her the way to handle it. Do you weave? Ah, you have the wool-spinner's hands. I will teach you. Do you live in Bath?"

"At—at Master Lucas's house. I—but don't tell anyone—"

"At Master Lucas's house? But I live near you. Open your back window and you will see. Yes, I will teach you to weave. You come to the back door, and—"

The front curtains were thrust open by the carter's whip.

"Hey, Butterbox. Here us be at Overbrook. You

make haste and hop out now." He pulled his horses to a standstill. "Out with that gear of yours now. A week today I'll be back, and bring you to Bath again, and if you've not taught Goodwife Jackson to weave on your newfangled loom by then, why, Goodman Jackson'll wonder what a pair of horns feels like, I'll be bound!"

"Goot-day, *mevrouw*," said Pieter very soberly, as the wagon went on its way. Alison watched him out of sight as far as she could see. Valentine's Day it was. . . .

She was still in thought when the cart drew up at Spinners Hill.

"Here you be, lass. Get down." The carter helped her out. "There. Now my shilling."

"Oh. . . ." She unfastened the chain under her dress and held it out to him. "Here's all I have."

He drew back. "What's this? I can't take this, my dear. 'Tis gold, and worth twenty crowns. I can't take it."

"Oh go on. It's not stolen, it's my own."

"That's as may be, but there! You don't expect me to take a thing like that for a shilling's riding? Put it away, my girl. There, I'll give you the ride for the love of God, and welcome."

"Why—thank you—thank you—" and she clumsily began putting the chain on again. "You're very good."

"It's what I'd do for any pretty lass—" He looked at her more closely, "Eh, now I know who you are. You're Master Lucas's young widow, now, bain't you?"

She paled a little. "What if I am?"

"Nothing, nothing—Oh, you can trust me, my pretty. I'll say nothing to nobody."

"And I should think not!" she retorted. "Why should you? I've only come to see my godsib Alison Barton, who lives by Spinners Hill—what's that to tell anyone?"

He grinned. "Oh ay, my dear, a pretty story—so it's your godsib, is it? A pretty story, but my mouth bain't so wide as to swallow it. Here's Valentine's Day come, and a pretty lass steals out of doors on the quiet, and ready to give her last gaudy to the carter for an hour's ride—and all to see her godsib! No, no, that cock won't fight, my dear—"

She reddened, angry and worried. "Oh, you stupid man, I tell you it's the truth. If I told you a lie you'd believe me."

"Maybe I would, if 'twere a better one than that. But no matter—I'll keep your counsel. I won't blab."

". . . Much," thought Alison with considerable resentment, as she saw him lumber away down the hill. The old tale-carrier—all up and down the country, from parish to parish, with his tongue wagging like a hound's tail. Her heart sank. And not as if there were any truth in it either—only his own filthy mind—

No matter. She shrugged her shoulders and set off over the fields that divided her from godsib Alison's house.

Alison Barton was a "deye"—that is, a small dairy farmer. Her husband, Wat Barton, a quiet unambitious man, owned a small holding, very small indeed, and kept himself going in his little cottage by digging his kail-yard, keeping his pig, his cow, and his poaching dog; and so he might have gone on, just living off his land, but his wife had ideas in her own quiet way, and what with the butter, the cream, and the cheese (increasing his one cow to two, and then to three) and what with her bees, and her hens, and her geese, she had worked up a snug little trade, and carried handsomer coifs on her head of a Sunday than Dame Prout herself. They had no children, and within their modest limits they lived very comfortably.

The place stank of farm manure, of course—to Alison's senses a cheerful and homelike smell. Master Lucas's house was always sweet with lavender, rosewater, beeswax and cedarwood—but that was the smell of bondage. This was far better. And as soon as she had set her pattens on the oozing muck of the yard, there came godsib Alison flying out of the door, with her arms outstretched in welcome.

"Alison—God bless you, child!"

"Alison—oh, my dear godsib!"

They fell into each other's arms, laughing and crying and making an enjoyable fuss of one another.

"Come in by the hearth, my love—why, it's years—how did 'ee get here? Come away in—let's look at 'ee—oh, dear heart alive, you're pinched and pale—quite fallen all away—dear, dear—"

She led her in over the yard, and into the dark smoky little house-place; found her a seat on the settle, propped her back with cushions, and set a bowl of hot milk at her elbow.

"And well now, child, tell me what brings you here?"

"Oh, Alison—" For a moment she stared, seeking for words; then tears and words came together. "Oh, Alison, my dear life, I'm so wretched. I'm so unhappy, Alison. Oh, my life isn't worth living. I wish I could die. Honest to God I do. . . . If it wasn't for Gilbert, Alison, as God's my witness I'd throw myself into a river and end it all."

"My dear, my dear." Alison's big red hand stroked little Alison's tawny hair. "Tell me, then. It's those bitches of stepdaughters of yours, I'll be bound. As ill-conditioned a pair of shrews as ever I saw. Oh, if I could have the whipping of them! What have they done this time?"

"It's what they always do—Oh, godsib, when Lucas was my husband 'twas bad enough, but give him his due, he was kind to me in his fashion, and wouldn't let they two oppress me; but now they're forever at me. I'm their slave day and night—I'm less than the hired girl—and my poor Gilbert, they flout him and fleer at him, and bob and knock and pinch him, and call him—ill names. . . ."

The godsib nodded, her big understanding eyes fixed on Alison's tearful ones. "I know, love. A miserable pair they be. No wonder you look pale and whisht. Did the old man leave you money, now?"

"Twenty pounds a year, at their sole dispense—and fare, board and bed, on condition that I don't marry again—that's his bounty."

"Then," said Alison the elder, setting down the empty milk-bowl, and leaning back against the wood of the settle, "it's clear what you must do, godchild, you must marry again."

"What!"

"Yes, love. You must marry again."

She was a fine hearty woman, was Alison Barton, not more than forty, with jet-black hair, weather-beaten rosy cheeks, and all her teeth sound in her head. Now, leaning against the settle in the firelight, she laughed back confidently at young Alison's dismayed face.

"It's truth, love. The way things are, a woman can't do nought without a man—you've got to have a man, some way, to do things for ye—though, by the Mass, there isn't much a man can do for me that I can't do for myself, barring only—well, let that pass." She sniggered. "No, but listen, love. I know you—I've known you since your chrisom day, no less—and you're a bold spirit, that wants to do and be and live on your own, and not wait for a man to pick apples for you when you can climb you own trees. Well, in a measure, so'm I. But see here—I took honest Wat, who's a kind easy man, though no beauty. Now I've a man with a strong arm to mind me, and I've got my own little trade—the milk and cream, and the cheese and eggs and honey—God knows I work hard, but don't I reap the fruit of my hands? See this gown? Look,"—she threw open a chest in a dark corner—"here's a coif to put on any Sunday, and here's another. Did I have to ask Wat for them? Not I. Mind you, he'll buy me a pair of beads a time or two, but isn't it good to go and get just what you want, and ask no one?"

Alison sighed sharply.

"Oh God—but how could I do that?"

"I don't know, love, but we'll think of something. All men have talents, the Gospels say, don't they? and we have to make the five into ten.—Come now—what you want to find is a good easy husband, like my Wat. Think, child. Lucas was no choosing of yours, but this time you can pick and choose to suit yourself. One with no curst daughters, or other kindred to vex you. One richer than old Lucas—yes, and one who'd be

71

kind to little Gilbert. With your looks, you can have all the men in the town to choose from—hey-ho, some women'd give their ears to have your luck. What d'ye say?''

Alison looked down, twisting her hands in her lap.

''I—I don't think I like being married. I don't—care for—men.''

''Meaning you don't want a man to your bed? Rubbish, child. There's men and men. That doting old Lucas, now, he was no good to any woman. But there's others that are otherwise—''

She dropped her voice, and leaned forward, looking into Alison's face.

''Tell me, now—who was Gilbert's father?''

Alison gasped.

''I—I—didn't think anyone knew—''

''Your mother said it was a friar—''

''Friar? God forbid! No, it was—it was—''

And rather shakily and incoherently, Alison told her the whole story.

Alison the elder wept at the end of the tale, being deeply sentimental.

''And so you never saw him again? Ay, I know—it's the way men do, and one never knows why. But you never learnt more of his name than just Gilbert—nor his quality, nor his kindred?—No, but there, what maid thinks of that, when she's. . . . Why, child, he might have been some great nobleman travelling unknown.''

''I think not,'' said Alison the younger, even then sturdily realistic. ''He seemed like a yeoman's son.''

''Oh well, belike, belike. Maybe from the other side of the country—or a sea captain from Bristol—''

''Anyway,'' said young Alison, ''he's gone. Why

did he never send me word or token? But he'd never find me now."

"Did you love him, my dear?"

"Oh, Alison—if you knew. . . . If I could find him now. . . ."

"Yes, there were a man to marry. But there's other men in the world, my dear, plenty of men to choose from, and some you'd fancy. . . . Oh, I know. I know. You've been the poor bondmaid long enough—Patient Grissell, like the old tale your grandmother used to tell—but manage things well now, you can have all the men your servants, and be your own mistress too."

She rose from the settle and began going methodically about the housework. Alison sat staring into the fire. The fire warmed her, and her thoughts began to be warming too. Yes, there could be ways and ways to do things—more ways of killing a dog than choking him with butter. . . . Talents, did she say? Well, what about weaving? That Hollander boy, now—he could teach her a thing or two with that new loom—and somehow the prospect of having his big brown hands over hers, and his broad chest at her back, and his brown-blond face just at her ear as he taught her, was more than a little breathtaking. . . .

Outside it was raining.

"By the way," said Alison the elder, "how be you to get back, my dear?"

"Oh—I don't know. I could walk, if the rain stops. I thought maybe there was some way—"

"You'll not walk. Wat will ride you back pillion on the mare. He'll be in soon. You'll take supper with us and then he'll ride you back."

A cat, depressed and bedraggled, left the settle corner and ran to the housewife where she was putting

73

meat into the pot. Alison the elder dropped a few good gobblets of meat for her.

"Why, it's Sukey—what's the matter with her, in God's name? The poor thing's sick, surely—"

"That was Adam," and a frown came over the mistress's face as she spoke. "Wat's hired man, the sour brute. He said that she went abroad too much, and caught no mice, and that he'd teach her to stay home by scalding her skin—so he flung a pan of boiling water at her. I sorted him! I scalded him worse with my tongue than he scalded poor Sukey—he won't do that again. But there she is, poor beast . . . because her fur's burnt off in patches, she feels too poor in herself to stir out o'nights, he thinks she's cured of roving. And why shouldn't she rove? She catches all the mice she needs, and if she gets kittens, there'll be that many more mousers . . . but there now—I've put butter and herb salve on her fur, and soon it will be healed and sleek again, and then she'll be out and about, and join the singing on the roof and show off her fine fur—won't 'ee, poor tibby?"

She bent down and gave the cat another piece of meat, and then came and sat on the settle by Alison, and put her arms round her.

"Godchild, you're a poor little scalded cat yourself. No matter—your fur will grow again, and then out you go once more and take your pleasure—and you'll be too wise to be scalded again. . . ."

"I wish I could learn some wisdom, godsib. Yet you tell me to marry again, and yet not be made a scalded cat once more . . . ?"

"Ways and ways, my dear. Think it over."

There was no means of telling the time in a cottage like the Bartons', save the vague and varying indication of the passing daylight, and rarely, far away and often not heard, the convent bell. The rain shut down heavily—it grew dark, and at last Wat came in, wet and tired, leading the mare, dead lame.

"There's no getting you home tonight," said Dame Barton. Alison's conscience smote her—her heart sank—she panicked, she wept—but nothing could be done. It was dark, it was raining torrentially, the mare couldn't go a step, nor could Wat Barton.

"In the devil's name," he growled, "what's the matter with a truckle bed at my wife's side, that you'd have a man turn out in the dark and the wet? It's ten miles into Bath, and raining like Noah's Flood—you'd not get a man to go out if it were to fetch the midwife. Be content now—those stepdaughters of yours can't murder you."

So Alison stayed the night, and Alison the elder plied her with mulled ale till she forgot about the sisters and went off to bed drowsy and warm and happy, with the rain making a little island of the cottage and her sleepy contentment.

But in the morning, the raw grey morning. . . . Still raining, the roads all miry—"I'll have to walk it," she said, "I daren't stay longer—" and her heart and stomach failed her, and she could hardly eat any breakfast.

"Heart up, my dear," urged her godmother. "If they beat thee, come back to us."

Alison sadly reflected how unlikely she was to get the least chance of doing so. She would be a prisoner now for good and all.

Ten miles to walk, over mire and muck, and stones and ruts, in the teeth of that rain and wind—and at the end of it, what a reception! How she longed to stay in the snug cottage, with its warmth and kindliness and its careless comfort—only a crushing and servile fear drove her out, and another fear lest her offence should be visited on poor little Gilbert.

She plodded out into the sighing lanes.

Oh, if only she had a protector—she and Gilbert—yes, a man, as godsib Alison said—there was something in the idea. A man to protect her, and to help her protect herself. Someone like Pieter the weaver—oh, if only Pieter the weaver was rich, and had a house and a position and a livelihood to offer her and Gilbert. A young, charming, gallant man, like those heroes of romances told by the firelight. . . .

Behind her in the lane she heard a horse. A horse meant a man. Now who? And would he give her a lift on his pillion? She did not look round, but tried to guess what kind of man it was. Then when she did look round, it was not upwards but downwards, at the horse's hoofs—which did not tell her much, except that it was a good horse and well-kept.

A voice hailed her.

"Why, Mistress Lucas! Where are you going this foul wet day, and all alone? Can I take you anywhere?"

It was Master Watkyn the lawyer.

Seated not behind Master Watkyn, but on his saddle-bow before him, she considered him at close quarters. For the moment she certainly felt safe, looked after, escorted, protected. His body, lean but well-knit for his age, shielded her from the wet wind. He had a clean and cheerful face, and when his official manner was laid aside he had a twinkle in his eye. He talked to her kindly, encouragingly, and very soon she was chatting to him like a child, and telling him her troubles.

"Mistress," he said, and his arm gathered her closer to him, "I'll give you my solemn counsel as a man of law. You have a remedy at hand for all your discontents. You should marry again."

She gasped a little, and the blood came into her cheeks. "What, me?"

"Why not? You're young—you're—permit me to say it, mistress, very handsome. You've but the one child, and he's a pleasant enough little rogue." A tear came into Alison's eyes at this—it was so seldom anyone spoke kindly of poor Gilbert. "And here am I, mistress, a widowed man without a child, and no kin in the world that trouble me at all—a house and money and all a woman could desire. . . ."

She drew back in his arms and looked up into his face.

"Oh, I'm not a young fellow, lass—but there, I'm but fifty, and your Lucas was nearer seventy. If you knew, my lass, how my heart beats when I put my arms round you—thus—"

He laughed.

"As if I were a boy of twenty, when I look down at your red lips. . . . Old Lucas was no husband to you. I'd grow younger every day with you—a man must forget his books and his parchments sometimes—Oh, blessed God, how you madden a man. . . . Pretty, pretty little mistress Alison, marry me and let me make you happy—"

Here it was. Now she could walk in upon those grim sisters and say, "I'm to marry Master Watkyn, and you can do what you please with your bed and board and your lousy twenty pounds—and if you lay your stick to me I'll run to him straight—"

They were riding into the town. There was the roof of the house where the Netherlanders lived—and the gable window, and Pieter sitting with his back to her, weaving—but what was the use of thinking about Pieter? There was her home coming in sight, her prison, her place of judgement.

She lifted her face, as demure as a little maiden at catechism.

"Oh yes, if you please, Master Watkyn."

Her dewy innocence took his breath away. He hugged her to him like a bear, and roared with laughter.

Now indeed little Alison's life was changed—translated at one step from hell to heaven. The dismay and indignation of the sisters was pure delight to her—their shocked faces, first pale, then red, and at last almost purple with zealous denunciation—their final gesture of repudiation of the shameless creature—and most of all, Alison's private knowledge that Catherine herself had unsuccessfully tried to capture that same wealthy widower.

The wedding was a quiet affair this time, but Watkyn brought over Alison's father and mother from Watchet at his own expense and lodged them for several days. This was the first time she had seen them since Gilbert's christening, and she could not have appreciated anything more deeply.

She had money now, more money than she had ever known in her life—though not more than she knew what to do with. Not that she was extravagant—her bitter apprenticeship had taught her how to do without money, and her natural shrewdness made her manage what she had as if she might never have any more. Master Watkyn was comfortably well off, though not inordinately rich; hardly as rich as Lucas had been, but he had better ideas as to the use of his money. He was far from mean, and liked to taste the fruit of his labours; and he had no one to spend his money on but Alison. She never forgot the thrill when he first placed a purse of gold pieces in her hands, and bade her go buy herself gowns and linen; and afterwards showed himself pleased with her choice, which was suitable enough—not the heavy dragging petticoats that the Lucas sisters had thrust upon her, but yet nothing too light and tawdry—rich soft stuffs, fine-textured and of sweet colours, for already she was a judge of such things; and crisp white neckerchiefs and coifs, from which her bonny face blossomed out clean and fresh, with a new bloom of happiness on her cheeks, and sparkle in her eyes.

She learnt, too, the delight of being mistress in her own house—her own kitchen, linen-closet, and garden, where she could make her own choice and her own mistakes, and pay for them too, with no one to dictate to her; the new bunch of keys at her girdle really represented something now—power and authority and dignity.

And Gilbert grew and flourished; Watkyn, whose only child had been the poor stillborn baby that brought his first wife to her grave, took the little red-headed urchin to his heart, and asked no questions about his colour—after all, was not Alison's hair red? Gilbert took to calling him father, and loved him as he never could have loved Lucas. Watkyn found a nurse for him, too, as he grew bigger, so that Alison should not be overburdened—partly because he clung to the hope that she might soon bear him another child.

And as a lover? Well . . .

He was deeply affectionate, touchingly, desperately passionate; he would caress her with tears in his eyes, blessing her, and swearing she gave him back his lost youth. For a man of fifty he was reasonably virile, and she began for the first time to be aware of pleasure in marriage; but as he was not Lucas, so equally he was not Gilbert, her first love, to whom her thoughts turned more than ever now that she could imagine what might have been. . . .

But she was happy, her life was full, and summer smiled upon them; and the ugly sisters gnashed their teeth in outer darkness.

But it is only the elderly that can move smoothly towards the inevitable sunset.

Watkyn's joyful rejuvenation could not last long. A year of perpetual honeymoon, and a year of tranquil glowing—and then it seemed that he had reached an end. His new toy no longer aroused the same delight. The dusty preoccupations of his business claimed him back. He grew grave and unresponsive, and forgot to play at being young. Had Alison indeed borne him a child, perhaps the new interest would have stimulated him again; but she did not, and the chances of her doing so became more remote. And Alison, inevitably, began to find him boring.

She was finding her life boring, too; it was too easy, the house ran itself with the menservants and maidservants, there was no more interest to be got out of it—hers was not the temperament to multiply ornaments and repolish the polished surfaces, nor did she care a great deal for the stillroom. Gilbert was busy on his own devices, and would soon be learning his lessons at the Abbey—she could not see herself teaching him his hornbook—remembering her own struggles, she could not imagine any other way of teaching letters but with beating, and as she would not do that to him, why then she couldn't teach him his letters. And anyhow that was not what she wanted to do. She wanted an art of her own.

"I want a loom," she told Watkyn. "One of those new looms like Mistress Jones has—the Flemish style. Wilt thou buy me a fine new loom, and yarn to weave?"

"Why, sweetheart," he said, looking up from his manuscripts with a tired elderly smile, "what dost thou want a loom for? I can buy thee all the cloth thou'st need."

"Yes, but—it's for something to do. I'm overmuch idle. I was good at it, thou knows. Let me, let me, husband dear! I'll weave thee stuff for the best suit thee ever had . . . do, do, do!"

"As you will, my chuck. But thou'lt need to learn the way of these new looms. Why not get Hans Butterbox—what's his name, Pieter the Fleming, over the way, to teach thee? I'll pay him. Do so, my love—it will keep thee out of mischief."

If her heart thumped for just a second, just once or twice, it was because the name of Dutch Pieter had taken her off her guard. . . . Truly and sincerely, she had not wished it. And when she went over to his house, later that very day, she intended nothing more than to learn the Flemish style of weaving, to improve her craft and to pass the time.

As Pieter turned from his loom in the low-roofed shed, he saw her standing in the doorway—it was the

81

first bright day of April and she was framed among daffodils and pear-blossom, with pigeons fluttering behind her head—and she herself was all spring and blossoms, with her dainty pearl-grey dress and her fresh kerchief, her red-gold hair and her golden-rose face.

He gasped, and took one step towards her, and then stopped. "Oh, milady—" His big blue eyes were fixed upon her, overcome. He found hesitant words. "You have come—to me?" She thought he was about to fall on his knees.

For a moment the spell touched her also, but she shook it off, was brisk and businesslike.

"I've come to take lessons from you, Master Pieter. I want to learn the Flemish way of weaving. Will you teach me?"

"Oh, mistress—milady—*mevrouw*." Still he could not muster his words.

"My husband," she brought out the words deliberately, "will pay you well. Will you teach me?"

"Oh, yes, yes." He exhaled a long breath. "I will teach you, *mevrouw*. I will teach you for no money."

"What, for no money at all? For love?" She forced her tone to be light.

"Why, yes, I will teach you for . . ."

She waited and he avoided her eye.

"For no money. Come, sit down and I will show you."

So she took her place at the loom, and as she had imagined it, he leant over her shoulder, and his big brown hands guided hers. And she forced herself to pay attention to the work, for really, truly, genuinely, that was all she had come for.

FOUR

Weaving

SO the summer went on, and poor Watkyn was beyond all doubt a sick man. He grew thinner, he wasted and withered, grey in the face as well as the hair; he ate and drank vastly, but got no fatter; an inward sickness which no doctor could understand was gnawing him away. He lost interest in everything, save to mope over a few old manuscripts, and to pace his garden melancholy-wise. He was still gentle and considerate to Alison, and still generous, but he was sad company; and his brief passion had long burnt itself out, leaving only a respectful tenderness more suited to a grandmother. So Alison would lie night after night stretched out tensely in the great double bed, waiting for the caresses that never came. And seeing the shuttle go to and fro, and the patterns of the warp and woof forming and re-forming, and the shuttle saying to her "Shall I—shan't I—should I—shouldn't I?" hour after hour, and night after night.

Every kind of way, she turned it over in her mind. What would godsib Alison say? Oh yes, she knew what godsib Alison would say—why, of course—something about nobody missing a slice from a cut loaf. . . .

She worked away eagerly at her weaving; it was something to keep her mind and her hands occupied, and it was a bond of pleasure between her and Pieter—a kind of music they made together. She wove beautiful cloth under his tuition, broadcloths and brocades and velvets, taffetas and Holland linen. And so the summer went on, piling up the tension for the thunderbreak. . . .

It was a very hot afternoon—outside, below the loft where they now worked so as not to disturb Pieter's relatives with the sound of the looms, the hum of bees came up, the croodling of doves, and the monotonous mutter of Pieter's father in the room across the courtyard, reading the Bible in Flemish to Pieter's mother and three old uncles. The sunlight reflected off the white wall through the gable that led into the loft, and a red rosebriar lay sprawled across the wall. Inside, the loft was dark and cooler than outside—but Alison suddenly let her hands drop from the loom.

"Oh God, Pieter, I'm tired—"

He put his arm round her and led her to the far corner of the loft, where there was a pile of woven cloth and bales of wool—a deep, soft bed. With a little gasp of weariness she sank into this, and he crouched beside her, looking—looking at her face.

"Pieter—oh, you strange boy, you're crying."

"I—" he spoke in his funny, hesitant way. "I am sorry for you, Elsa—so very sorry."

"Yes—why?" she said it with a soft breathlessness, not moving, her eyes fixed on his eyes.

"Oh, you are not happy. Elsa, Elsa—you are a beautiful rose that no one will pluck, a beautiful peach that no one will eat."

Instead of saying "What do you mean?" she said, "How did you guess?"

"I know. I feel everything you feel. Do you think I do not know? It is—all round you, cold, fever, hungry, suffering—what can I say? And so beautiful—oh, you must not be so sad, you must not suffer, you must not—"

His arms were round her.

"What of yourself, Pieter? You're unhappy too—"

"Me? Ach, my God, Elsa, not of me I speak! But you—oh, my beloved—it is for you, my tears—"

His head was between her breasts, and suddenly she was reminded of Gilbert—not Gilbert the man, but Gilbert her own baby. She bent her lips to his golden hair. Feeling her touch, he uttered a strange wild cry—lifted his face to hers, and gathered her into a fierce embrace. . . .

And this at last was what life had been owing her. The quiet purr of the doves, the sunlight on the wall outside, the wafting scent of the roses—all drowsy and happy and contented. So they remained, until the white sunlight turned to amber and then to red, and the doves fluttered as the evening breeze cooled; and Pieter kissed her gravely, and bade her farewell, finger on lip. And she went back, not guiltily, but as one carrying a precious secret, withdrawn into herself lest she betray her treasure.

From this time onward Alison ceased to lie awake

longing for Gilbert; she slept remarkably soundly, and woke each morning to a strange and rather exciting mixture of emotions.

She had a lover now, and such a lover! She could feel a secret pride when she watched him from her window as he walked down the street; she wished she could be seen with him, that she dared to tell other women, "This man is mine." But since she might not, it was like wearing a beautiful jewel under her dress. They would envy her if they knew, those smug damsels of Bath, and meantime she envied none of them.

She was a woman now, complete and fulfilled, used and appreciated as a woman should be; her own body, as well as her heart, had taught her secrets of pleasure she had not known before, and was enhanced and made full of meaning. Every part of her became precious to herself, because he held it precious.

But—she was a very wicked girl. She was deceiving her husband, her poor old kind sick husband. Oh yes, she was, and the men would call him a shameful name if they knew. If they knew!—But nobody knew, so nobody could make him ashamed—poor old Watkyn, she didn't want to hurt him, and she would never let him know. She was true to him, anyway, for all practical purposes—there she was whenever he wanted her—at his table, and (oh, dear God!) in his bed, for all the good that was. It was only in the long, long hours of the daytime, when he left her alone, and sat in his closet, studying, wrapped in a long thick robe to keep himself warm, or perhaps in his small parlour with his clients or his colleagues, talking over remote points of law—in the hours that he gave to all dusty matters, and never cared or knew if his wife were there or a hundred miles away—only then it was that those stolen meetings took place, those moments of intimate pleasure in the dark corner of the weaving loft, among the wool-bales. Pieter found a way to set the loom swinging and rattling for quite a long time together, so that the absence of the wonted noise would not be too noticeable. . . .

Sometimes she asked herself—supposing she became pregnant? Well, of course, Watkyn would be only too delighted—provided he could be convinced that it was his. That, at present, was a little unlikely—no matter, if the emergency arose she would find means, no doubt, to make the thing seem credible.

If only she had had some such recourse when she was tied to old Lucas, how much more tolerable life would have been . . . and now, poor old Watkyn was fast becoming as bad as old Lucas. Anyhow, she was determined never to be without love again. With Lucas, of course, she never could have made any such escape, because of the sisters.

The sisters! Odd to think of them now. She had cut adrift from them entirely since she married Watkyn, and never spoke to them, though she frequently saw them going up and down the town, and especially in church, where she could not avoid meeting them and giving them a formal greeting.

Strange to think she had two stepdaughters—yes, stepdaughters! Old enough to be her mother, and never exchanging a word with her. . . .

It was one fine morning when she was walking briskly down to her daily tryst at the weaving loft, when in a narrow cobbled passageway she came face to face with Catherine, the younger of the two sisters.

"Oh—goodmorrow, *Mistress* Watkyn," said Catherine, with just a little sneering emphasis on the title.

"Oh—goodmorrow, ma'am, I'm sure," Alison replied with elaborate politeness, dropping her a curtsey.

"And where might you be going?"

"I'm going weaving, so please you," said Alison, looking her straight in the face.

The other's eyes snapped.

"Indeed? Yes—I hear you do a deal of weaving, a very great deal of weaving, these days. Weaving a fine web of trouble, I'll say."

"I don't know what you mean," said Alison—but for the life of her she could not stop the dreadful betraying blush that spread all over her face.

"I'll wager you do—and it's time your poor deluded fool of a husband did. Do you blush? You'll blush more when you get your deserts—lucky for you if you escape whipping at the tail of a cart. . . . I've told you now, so mind yourself. I always knew how it would be."

Alison might have said, "Mind your own business," or she might have said, "Prove it if you can," but she was too taken aback to say anything. She only stood, red-faced and confounded, while Catherine swept her skirt aside from her, and passing her with a gloating look, flounced away down the slope.

Alison could not turn and run for home—she was afraid of going on to Pieter's house, but to turn back would mean walking behind Catherine, and making her aware of her retreat. She must needs go on the way she was going—perhaps she could turn down a side way, and go back? But no—anyone who saw her would notice that she had changed her mind, and would guess why—anyone who was watching from a window or a door, a roof or a chimney—she had thought herself so secure before, and now there were eyes everywhere.

It was Watkyn she worried about most. Those smug burgesses of Bath, she hated them anyway—let them spit on her, she'd spit back—but poor old Watkyn—that he should learn such a thing from her enemies, that they should tell him this to break his heart—she could not bear it. He had been so kind to her, and in a way she was very fond of him. He must not suffer this blow. No, not even if it meant giving up Pieter.

Since she could do nothing else, she hastened on towards the Flemings' house, and climbed the ladder into the loft; as ever, he was waiting there for her, and caught her in his arms as she stepped through the gable. But she thrust him away from her, and wept.

"What is the matter, my dear? You weep? Ah, why for?"

"Pieter, we must part. I mustn't come here anymore. They—they know, Pieter."

"Who knows, my love?"

"Catherine—my stepdaughter. And Elizabeth, the other one. And by now, all their godsibs and acquaintances. And soon everyone in Bath, and—my husband too."

"No?" he dropped the syllable deeply and softly.

"Yes—I met Catherine, the bitch, and she taxed me with it—and I, like a fool, could do nothing but blush. . . . Pieter, it is finished. My poor husband, don't you see? I can't hurt him."

"Why, my dear—" he smiled sadly—"It is of you this concerns, not your husband. He does not love you—why then—"

"No matter for that, dearest. He doesn't love me, and yet he loves me, and he's been good to me, and I can't break his heart. I have only come here to say—ah, I can't say it. . . ."

"To say what, my sweet, sweet Elsa?"

"To say—goodbye."

"Ah, no, no . . . but yes," he lowered his eyes. "You are right. It is for the danger to you. We must say goodbye, then. But say goodbye—in my arms."

"Once more, dear Pieter—only once. . . ."

She sat up among the wool-bales.

"What's that noise below?"

"Keep still," said Pieter. "Make no sound. Listen."

Footsteps, and then a loud knocking on the door of the shed below the loft.

"Don't answer," whispered Pieter.

Alison's heart pounded with fear. A voice called.

"Mistress Watkyn! Mistress Watkyn! Is Mistress Watkyn there?"

"Oh, my God!" Alison muttered. "They've found us!"

"Keep hidden," said Peter. "Who is that?"

"It's Joan, my maid."

The voice began again, not angry, but with entreaty.

"Oh, Mistress Watkyn, if you be there, come down quick!"

Alison struggled to her feet, putting her dress in order, and came with as firm a step as she could to the gable entrance.

"Well, I'm here—what is it, Joan?"

"Oh, Mistress—come at once to the master—he's dying."

*　　*　　*

He was in a deep and death-like coma, hardly breathing. Martin, the house-man, had found him in his reading-closet, slumped against the door in his velvet gown, as he had fallen, his book in his hands. When Alison saw him, he was laid on the bed as if already stretched out for his grave. She flung herself on her knees by him in a passion of weeping.

Presently she roused herself, for people were coming in—all sorts of friends, neighbours, kinsfolk—the doctor, the barber, the apothecary—all looking, and peering, and shaking their heads. The doctor pronounced that life was still in him, but what could be done for a man in the death-sleep? They bled him and cupped him, slapped his cheeks, rubbed his limbs, burnt feathers under his nose, put irons to his feet. They also prayed. . . .

When the doctor opened the vein, the blood flowed, showing that he was still alive; but he neither stirred nor woke. All this while Alison stood by the bed-foot, watching him intently, her tears dried into extreme seriousness.

The friends and relatives shuffled and pushed and crowded in and out of the room, around the big curtained bed. Suddenly Alison looked up, and there were Catherine and Elizabeth looking at her. Catherine raised her brows with wicked intention. Alison tried to look her full in the face, but felt herself trembling all over. Could Catherine, she thought in sudden panic, accuse her of having caused her husband's death?

She sat by his bedside almost without intermission, for three days and three nights, faithfully praying for him. At some moment during that time, he passed away, though none could be sure when; neither could they be sure that he was truly dead, till the signs of decay began to show. Then Alison, very quiet and self-contained, left his side, and the women prepared him for burial.

She comported herself throughout the days that followed with a correct and impeccable demeanour. She did not weep anymore, but put on her black, and followed his coffin with downcast eyes and steady pace, looking at no one. At his requiem she prayed fervently. Ought she, she wondered, to go to shrift and confess her fault? But no—not to one of those monks. . . . She prayed, and kept her prayers to herself; and took good care to put up candles for Watkyn, and pay for the masses, and give orders for a suitable monument.

And then, when a whole month had gone by, and his "month's mind" had been properly celebrated, she put on a cloak with a hood, and went down the street once more to the Flemings' house. Only to see Pieter, only to exchange a word with him—she had not seen him, all those days, for he had discreetly kept out of sight, and avoided even the funeral; but now, she just wanted to greet him, and say a final farewell to him, nothing more.

The loft door was shuttered and the ladder gone. She knocked on the door of the shed below, but no answer came. She knocked again.

A door opened in the adjoining house, and an ugly old Flemish serving-woman came out.

"He's gone away," she said gruffly.

"Master Pieter the weaver—?"

"Gone away, back to de Nederlands. Will you see Meester de Hooch, his fader?"

"Oh, no, no thank you," she said hastily, and backed away.

"He iss married," said the old woman gratuitously. "To his cousin in Ghant."

"Oh," said Alison blankly. "Thank you."

The old woman went inside and shut the door, and Alison pulled the hood over her head again, and walked slowly away. It had begun to rain, and she felt very cold, empty and tired.

FIVE

Third Husband

SPRING had come round again, and on a fine May morning, always a time of good omen for Alison, her brothers Adam and Gamelyn came riding into Bath.

Adam was blacker and bushier than ever; Gamelyn had his own way at last, since both parents had died in the winter, and he was now a sort of prentice to Adam on board his small wine-carrying vessel, plying to Bordeaux and sometimes further. He too had a beard now, but more Alison's colour—tawny to yellowish; and both men were pretty grimy and unkempt; their clothes were the nonchalant kind of mixture that is apt to characterize seamen without uniform, and they rode their stocky ponies very uncertainly, with a good deal of bucking, walloping and mutual back-chat.

They entered the town at a walking pace, looking

about them, for they were strangers to Bath; and reined up at the principal inn.

"Shall we wait for Harry?" asked Gamelyn as he dismounted.

"Wait for Harry? No!" rejoined Adam. "If he's not got the wit to find our sister's house by the same means as ourselves, let him go hang. He'll turn up. Come on now. Oh, pest take you, horse, why can't you answer your helm?"

Having moored, as it were, the horses, they entered the dark-ceilinged inn parlour, and called for ale. The landlady served them, a brisk cleanly woman with a pouting bosom and an impressive white apron. They drew her into conversation.

"And can you tell us, mistress, where is the house of Mistress Watkyn—her that was Mistress Lucas?"

The woman drew a sharp breath seeming to swell up with what she knew.

"Oh—" The woman drew the syllable out, swept her eyes and her hands around her, and commanded her audience. "Well—there's much been said about her. Very much. Myself I'd not believe the half of it, but there—you know she's a widow again?"

Again Adam winked at Gamelyn, and rejoined, "No? How's that, then?"

"Oh—back last September, poor Master Watkyn he died, all suddenly. Found him stretched out stone dead in his little closet, all alone—poor decent man, and God above knows he'd treated her like a queen. But there—if an old man marries a young wife, and he with a mint of money and she with none at all, what can you expect? Yes, there was talk, and myself I don't believe it, but who's to stop people talking?

Wouldn't a fresh young piece like that be glad to be rid of an old fellow more like her father? All his money, his house, his land—she gets them all.''

She paused and smacked her lips. Gamelyn was red in the face and sweating, but Adam nudged him and continued to look the woman enquiringly in the eyes.

"Of course, I'm sorry for her," the landlady went on. "What Christian wouldn't be? But there's some that won't give her good morning in the streets. She can't get a servant to stay in the house—after all, none can tell *how* the poor man died—'twas mighty convenient for her. Oh yes, the doctors said he'd been sick a long while—but there, he went off just in the nick of time for her ladyship—all the town knew the Dutch weaver was her paramour, and the maid that went to call her to her poor husband's bedside found them kissing among the wool-bales . . . people would say she found means that poor Watkyn shouldn't know, and whether it was leechcraft or witchcraft. . . ."

Adam jumped up so suddenly, banging his fist on the table, that the woman gave a scream and tottered back against the wall.

"That'll do! Woman, has no one ever told you that an evil slandering tongue is witchcraft and poison too? Keep your dirty mouth shut, or by the Lord's thunders I'll slice the nose off your face, d'you hear?"

"Oh—oh—oh—" the gasps came out thinly. "I—you said you were no kin of hers—"

"And if we weren't?—No more of this. Show us the way to her house, and then shut your trap."

"Yes, yes, captain . . . to the right, then left and right again, a house at the corner. . . ."

"Enough. There's money for your sour beer. Come on," and he and Gamelyn flung out of the door and strode away, both too full of emotion to speak to each other.

They found the house—a fine, opulent place, yet somehow desolate. The little garden before the door was unweeded, the shutters fronting the street were all closed, there was a lack of sparkle and life about it—a house where no one visited, no one looked out of the windows. They knocked loudly at the door, and after a long pause a grey-faced idiot-looking girl opened to them. They thrust past her, and upstairs into the front parlour overlooking the street—a rich room, but forsaken, with shutters over the windows, making it dark and close. The half-witted maid pottered up and half-heartedly opened one shutter to let the light in; then she pottered away again to call her mistress. They heard a door open further in the house, a few words, a sob and a quick running; and Alison came rushing in.

"Adam—Gamelyn—oh, too good to be true—oh, dear lads—let me cry a bit. . . ."

She laid her head on Gamelyn's shoulder. She was dressed in sad black, without even a scrap of lace or linen; a black coif hid her hair; her face was pale, and never, the brothers thought, had they seen her so down-hearted before.

"My poor Alison, things have gone hard with you. We've heard you were widowed again—"

"Not only that." She seated herself in the settle by the cold grate, that now had not even green branches in it, and drew Gamelyn down beside her, while Adam sat opposite her. "Oh, not only that. I've lost—everything."

In the midst of the evident wealth around her she said it, and Adam nodded, understanding.

"We heard, sister. But you needn't heed the evil tongues."

"I know, I know—but oh, lads—what's my life now? I can't go out, for the cold looks and cruel mouths they make at me. A woman drew her skirt aside once as I went by, as if I were something foul. No one comes to the house. No servants will stay with me—I know they think I'm a witch and a poisoner . . . and as God's my witness, I say, I never, never, never. . . ."

"I know, sweetheart," murmured Gamelyn, stroking her head under the black coif. "No need to tell us. We know thee couldn't have done any such thing. There, there, be calm."

"You must live, lass," said Adam. "After all's said, you must live. Courage and patience, my girl."

"I've tried to have courage and patience—but oh, God! And then amidst it all comes the news of our mother's death, and father's so soon after—oh, if I could have died too. . . . Adam, Gamelyn, my life's finished. My name's a scandal, and I'm pointed out as a strumpet. And—and—oh, it's true, it's true. I did love Pieter the Hollander, but poor Watkyn never knew—I never grieved him to his knowledge, nor would I ever—"

"Hush, my dear," Gamelyn laid his finger to her lips. "No need to tell us that. Your secret's your own, and we won't hear it—but we know you never harmed him, and that's all there is to it—"

"Yes, yes, but I'm shamed—I daren't show my

face—oh, couldn't I go into a nunnery and hide myself, and be out of the way of their looking and whispering—''

''Nunnery? God's pity!'' burst out Adam, and Gamelyn shook her gently by the shoulder, saying, ''You in a nunnery? You'd better!''

And then from the road below, through the gap in the one carelessly swinging half-shutter, came a voice at which the brothers stiffened up and listened.

''Hullo—hullo—within there!'' said the voice.

''Oh, God's nails!'' said Adam. ''It's Harry, and he's coming here.''

''Hullo — hullo — Adam — Gamelyn — you lousy rogues, let me in—''

''And he's as drunk as a piper,'' said Gamelyn, with such a concerned face that Alison could not help smiling.

''Who's that?'' she asked.

''Oh, it's Adam's chief mate on the ship, one Harry Hardiman—a—a good fellow, but a bit noisy—we can't do with him now, with you like this—''

''No, no,'' protested Alison. ''If he's your friend let him come up. It's a long time,'' she added, with a return of her old sparkle, ''since I saw a man merry with ale! Bring him, boys.''

She stood up, and the coif, loosened with the flinging of her head against Gamelyn's shoulder, fell off, and her tawny-golden hair streamed free over her black dress.

Adam opened the other half of the shutter, and called to someone below.

''Come up, then, Harry, but behave yourself, and don't make all that noise.''

* * *

A shout answered him, and footsteps on the stairs—and Harry strode into the room, stooping his head under the low lintel of the panelled doorway.

He was taller than Adam—indeed, in the low-ceilinged upper room he could only just stand upright, and his great shoulders filled the door-frame. His beard was black like Adam's, but finely shaped, balancing a fine brow and nose; his hair flowed back in waves from under the seaman's tasselled cap, and his eyebrows were so bushy that they almost turned round into his eyes; but those eyes, bold and grey and full, were not so easily quenched. He stood four-square in an enormous pair of sea-boots, and carried a bottle under each arm, which he carefully set down inside the door before he advanced upon Alison, like a ship of war under full press of sail and oar—both hands outstretched, engulfing hers, as he printed a bearded kiss on each of her cheeks.

He breathed deeply, and she heard him say, "My service to you, Mistress Alison," and then suddenly, "Your brothers told me you was handsome, but by God, you're a nonesuch!"

He looked up at the brothers' ominous silence, and encountered their shocked faces.

"Harry, Harry," said Adam, "remember yourself, man—this is a house of mourning."

"Oh"—the big man stepped back and hung his head like a boy. "Oh, pardon, mistress, I'm a thoughtless brute—I didn't know—"

But Alison laughed, albeit a little wildly.

"House of mourning, is it? Not now. I've mourned long enough—dear God and the saints, I've mourned nine months, and that's too long—I'll not mourn anymore. My brothers are here—" and with a gesture she included Harry in that number. "For God's sake let's be merry."

She flung the remaining shutters open, then came back and faced the three, drawing them together. "Come now, make me acquainted with your friend. If he's your friend he's mine." She struck on a little bell, and the grey-faced girl came to the door. "Doll, fetch glasses and the best wine we have. And send Master Gilbert here."

Gilbert came running in—a fine bright little boy of seven now, who willingly called the two big sailors uncle, and was ready enough to make the third and biggest one an uncle too.

Glasses were brought, and Harry insisted on pouring out rich strong wine from his two bottles, and after that they had to have Alison's wine as well. At the open window they drank and laughed, and presently fell to singing songs—Gamelyn finding a forgotten lute in a corner of the parlour, and twanging it after a fashion, and Harry sometimes tootling on a cane pipe he carried in his pocket, sometimes joining in the songs with an overpowering deep bass that made the glasses rattle. Alison was like a pent-up stream suddenly released, and no frolic was too wild for her now. People passed by in the street, and looked up at the window at the noise—she laughed from the window in their scandalized faces. They made a day of it, sending out for cooked meats, manchet bread, and of course more wine—and as the evening went on they lit candles and went on singing—they danced a foursome square-dance too, and Harry swept Alison off her feet in his arms, and when they sat down to rest she just naturally sat on his knee.

"Oh me," she gasped, as she saw the appalled white

faces of neighbours below turned up to the lighted window, "they'll think the place is become a bawdy-house."

"Let them think what they please, sweetheart," said Harry, with his lips close to her ear.

"They've thought evil of me long enough," she said—a little slurring in her speech. "Now let 'em think all they like—rot 'em."

"They'll not slander you anymore," said Gamelyn. "You'll not stay here one day longer. Come to Bristol with us."

"Yes, come to Bristol with us—I've a house there, and you can keep house for us while we're ashore," said Adam. "What say you—will you come, Al'se my girl?"

"I'll come," said Alison. Her eyes were wide and shining in the candlelight, her cheeks flushed, all pallor gone now, and her tawny hair tossed about her shoulders, mingling with Harry's coal-black locks.

"You'll keep house for us?" said Adam.

"You'll do no such thing," said Harry, holding her firmly. "You'll marry me. Will you, sweetheart? Will you? Say yes, or I'll—"

"What'll you do?"

He faced her open-mouthed and dumb, and she laughed and flicked the tip of his nose with her finger.

"Say yes, then."

"Yes, with all my heart," she said, and he gathered her up into a huge embrace and kissed her resoundingly.

"You hear that, you fellows? She's to marry me. Yes, I said she's to marry me. Here," and he pulled a great gold signet-ring off his finger and rather unsteadily thrust it onto hers, "now we're troth-plight. And now come on, let's to bed."

"Oh no!" With a rather shrill squeal she extricated herself from him and dodged behind her brothers. "Not yet—oh, my life, not yet!"

"Give over, Harry," said Adam. "You're drunk. Come on, you'll sleep between us two tonight—we'll look after him, sister. You get to bed. In the morning pack up what you can, and bring the boy too—we ride to Bristol. We'll find a priest in Bristol, Harry—and until then you'll have to wait."

And so Alison left Bath next day, in a blaze of lurid scandal—drunken sailors carousing all night in her house, dancing and singing and mocking the towns-folk, and finally carrying her off on horseback, her and that doubtful-born child of hers. And the Lucas sisters gloated—but that didn't bring any of the Watkyn fortune their way. The house was sold, the land rented, and all that was of value conveyed down by packhorse and wagon to Bristol—where Alison found herself, almost as in a dream, married to this loud-shouting, big, glorious fellow, whose lightest touch could send her pulses leaping and awaken all her senses to an intoxicated, unregenerate delight.

In Bristol there was a cheerful little house fronting on the quay, and here Alison, her two brothers, and her new husband set up a jolly, carefree household, better than anything she had ever known. Now she was the wife of loud-mouthed, hard-drinking, jovial Harry, and she discovered a new thing in herself. This was that Nature had gifted her with a remarkable quality of sexual responsiveness. Nobody had called it out before—Gilbert had had no chance; Lucas had been nothing but grief and weariness to her; Watkyn's brief passion was too soon spent; and Pieter's love had been too furtive and full of fear and strain. But now that she could give herself without misgiving, and with all her heart, she blossomed with all a woman's best attributes. "Do you know, my darling," Harry would say, lifting his flushed face from her pillow, "you have a wonderful talent."

"A talent, Harry? But talents are—why, a talent's a holy gift—like—like if I had wisdom, or a sweet voice—something to praise God with, or do good to men—"

He laughed, but there was earnestness in his tone.

"And who says you haven't a talent? Believe me, sweetheart—loving as we do, and taking our pleasure in this good thing the Lord made, we praise Him in our fashion, as Adam and Eve did in their innocence. God's mercy, my dear, I say my prayers from my heart every time I come into thy bed. And as for doing good to men—oh, my darling!" And with his voice shaking, he would once more drop his head between her breasts.

So it was hardly surprising that she bore him four children in six years. Neither was it surprising, conditions being as they were, that one of them, the third, died. It was God's will—she wept passionately for a time, then prayed, commended its little soul to God and Blessed Mary, and in a short time was pregnant again. All her children were boys—she would have liked a girl, but in spite of various old-wives' specifics, she never got her wish; though Harry was the better pleased with his noisy gang of men-children. She brought them up with a fine carelessness, and they

grew into as arrant a band of young hooligans as ever
terrorized Bristol, tumbling around the ships as soon
as they could walk, falling into the water, escaping
death a hundred times by the devil's own luck
—cursed, kicked, hauled before the Justice before
they were tall enough to see over his table, and very
soon unafraid of man, God or devil. Harry thrashed
them from time to time, whenever he happened to
come back from sea, and for the rest let them rip, and
laughed to think what fighters they would make.
Alison had little to do with educating them—in fact
they would hardly have let anyone do much "bringing
up" to them, once they were able to scramble out of
the house in a gang.

And so she went happily about her untidy and comfortable house, and up and down the bustling quayside
of Bristol—growing and ripening in beauty, even in
her frequent pregnancies. For even then she was
graceful, and carried her self well, without
self-consciousness or self-pity, with her weight well
back on her heels and her loose gown flowing. Harry
came back once from the Irish shore, and told her a
proverb he had learnt there: "The three most beautiful
sights in the world—a ship in full sail, a field of corn in
full ear, and a fair woman great with child." She
remembered to the end of her days how they had
laughed together over the saying, and how he had
stood back and looked her up and down, and had
called her his lovely ship, full freighted with his
treasure—and had caught her into his arms again, and
kissed and adored her.

In those days every man in Bristol would turn his
head as she went by; and it would hardly be true to say
she had eyes for none of them, for she always had an

eye for a fine man; but it went no further than the eyes. Not one of them could compare with her Harry, and she was all his. She had even forgotten about Gilbert, save as the sweet and far-away memory of one dead. If it had not been for the boy Gilbert, she would have forgotten about him altogether. Young Gilbert, going on into his teens, was always different from Harry's brood—sturdy and manly enough, but not quite so outrageous; golden whereas they were black, and rather more thickset where they were scrawny; somewhat gentler of voice and manner, and more intelligent, with a particular tenderness for his mother, to whom he felt he had some special tie that went beyond the claims of Mat, Robin, and Dick. He tried to keep them in order, and indeed they paid a certain amount of deference to him, such as they never did to anyone else. Harry was fond of him, and when he went away on his voyages would say to him, "Look after your mother, lad. You're my bailiff, see? And keep those ruffians of mine in order till I come back to see to 'em, won't you?"

For he was away a great deal; true, when they first came to Bristol he remained at home for a whole year, and lived carefree on Alison's money; but the next summer he and the brothers fitted out a ship, and were off and away; and from that time on, the summers were all coming and going—around the coast, and to Ireland, to Bordeaux and Dieppe; further afield to Lisbon and Cadiz; and sometimes even through the Pillars of Hercules, past the perilous shores of Tangier, and into the fabulous blue Mediterranean; even to gorgeous Venice itself, where all Asia came to the door. And he would come home with strange treasures—jewelled necklaces and ear-rings, silks and

velvets that sent Alison into raptures at their cunning
workmanship—spices which made them all cough and
splutter when she tried them on their food—feathers of
outlandish birds, and once even a poor little monkey,
which she cherished and cossetted as if it had been a
child, in spite of its biting and scratching, from August
to November, when it died of coughing in its nest of
blankets.

In the winter there was no more seafaring, and
Harry and the brothers would rest at home, rich
enough for the time being, and plan future voyages;
and Harry would talk to Alison by the fire, and
promise that next year they would take her with them,
and she should see it all for herself—Tangier and Holy
Rome, and Venice and Alexandria, and even
Jerusalem and the blessed Sepulchre of the Lord. It
could be done, and plenty of women did it. Alison's
heart would leap as she gazed into the fire, and saw the
tawny desert and the palms—orange groves and
temples—lovely white heathen places on odorous
islands—tall men in white robes riding on camels—the
Nile and its magicians—India and the Mountains of
the Moon, and the Old Man of the Mountains alone in
a cave playing with handfuls of pearls and rubies. . . .

But always when the spring came and the ship was
fitted out, Alison was in full sail again for her own personal voyage, and Harry shook his head. "Too
precious a cargo for my ship, sweetheart," he said.
"But next year, surely." And so the years went on,
and Alison never crossed the seas at all.

She was passionately faithful to him—as for him, it
had come to her slowly over the second or third year
of her marriage that if he was hers alone when home
with her, that was his fashion of faithfulness. After a

while she came to fit into the pattern of her life the idea that he must have his various loves all over the world, and so long as he was still her ardent lover, she need not feel the poorer. So she would listen while he told her about Giacomina in Naples, and Baykal in Cyprus, and Fatimah in Tunis, and Elle in Athens—and she would tease him, and ask him intimate questions about them which ought to have embarrassed him but did not—and then laugh and let him carry her upstairs to bed. Indeed, she felt like the head queen of some rich Sultan's seraglio, supreme above all the world's beauties.

Most winter evenings he would spend an hour or two in the tavern, and then come home, cheerful enough but certainly not drunk; and while he was out she would push her loom out into the firelight, and go on with her weaving. Adam and Gamelyn were both married now, and lived with their wives in houses of their own; so she had time on her hands for weaving. She had begun to sell her cloth, too, and put by a gold piece here and there for her own private hoard. One might need it—Harry was a cheerful spendthrift, easy come easy go, and nobody's purse was bottomless— so away in a little wooden coffer behind a panel she put crown after crown, and kept her counsel about it.

So she sat by her loom, remembering the story her grandmother used to tell them about one Penelope who wove a web, and half listening for Harry. There was his step—several people walking together—no, two—

On an impulse she rose from the loom and put her eye to the little heart-shaped hole in the window shutter. Outside it was moonlight, and there was Harry, and—yes, a girl's shape beside him. Alison saw him pull her towards him and kiss her. She did not wait to see any more, but went shakenly back to the loom and sat down. It was nothing, of course—why should it be anything? If he had his Elles and Baykals in the Mediterranean, and she didn't mind, why shouldn't he kiss a girl here in Bristol?—And why should it be any more than a kiss?

The door opened, and Harry breezed in, without a look of guilt. Alison shook off her uneasiness, and went to welcome him with as merry a look as she could put on. She would not tax him with it—not yet.

Not yet—and so it went on.

First one little incident, then another.

Neighbours whispering—Adam's wife, and even Gamelyn's, anxious to tell her things she ought to know. A girl from the tavern, some said. Another said a hosier's wife at the other end of the town. Another said it was Custance Bell, the corn-chandler's daughter.

The spring weather should have sent Harry off to sea again, but he broke his ankle one day while going about the fitting-yards, and was laid up for weeks, and when the sailing season began he was still not able-bodied enough to sail, and stayed at home, disappointed and ill-tempered. The youngest boy was three years old, and this spring there was no further baby on the way. Bitterly Alison pondered that this would have been her chance for the voyage she so desired, but now it was out of the question. She waited on her lame man—but as soon as he was getting about with a stick, he was off and away to the *Red Lion*. Yes, it was Dorothy the serving-girl, right enough. Dorothy! What a choice!

Alison had gone out to the market one bright morning, and came back earlier than she had meant. She came back into the house, set down her basket, and mounted the little stairs to her bedchamber. There she stopped. Across her pillow, like a slashing bloodstain, lay a red ribbon. A red ribbon from a woman's hair. She had no red ribbons. . . . Her own bed . . .

She rushed downstairs. Bewildered, shaken and utterly tongue-tied. What should she do? Shriek and rave—call the neighbours to hear her shame? Let them all be witnesses that she could no longer deny it—that she was dethroned, humiliated, uncrowned?—Or whisper her bitterness—to whom? Gamelyn perhaps, but he was away at sea now. No one else—no, she must keep her lips shut, and eat her heart in silence. Almost mechanically she put on her cloak again, picked up her basket, and went out to walk—anywhere, anywhere, just to breathe the free air and keep moving till calmness should come back to her. . . .

Her steps led her to the quay; and there was a ship putting out. The vessel was already well away from the quayside, being warped out by two rowing-boats; the sails were gently filling, and soon she would be moving under her own power. The beauty of the sight woke Alison a little from her misery, and she watched as the ship slid into the channel. Then a man came out and stood on the sternworks, and a cry broke from Alison's lips. It was Gilbert. There was no mistaking him. Fifteen years older, and he was broader and tougher, and had a little bristling beard, but it was he, and no one else.

Without a thought, she cried as loud as she could,

"Gilbert—oh Gilbert! My love, Gilbert—don't you know me?"

He looked, and his face was lighted up with immense surprise.

"Why, my dear—" She could only just hear his voice as the ship carried him fast away from her.

"Gilbert—come back—"

Now she could only see his lips moving soundlessly.

Then she shrieked as a heavy hand fell on her shoulder from behind.

"God's nails, woman, what's this?" It was Harry, in a jealous fury. He flung her round to face him.

"Fine doings—my precious wife, waving to some lecherous dog of a sailor, and shouting after him like any strumpet along the sea front—Come you home, madam, and I'll thrash the white skin off your shoulders—"

She looked up at him—she had known mock-scoldings before, and had taken them all in good part, but there was no laughter in his eyes now. He was in a royal rage, a killing rage. But she braced herself to stand up to him.

"Is that so? You're a fine one to talk. Whose red ribbon was it I found on my bed—on my very bed, not half an hour ago? Tell me that before you beat me, you false villain—"

A crowd had begun to collect, stepping over the cobblestones and coils of rope, and standing in and out of boats and fishing nets.

"Oh, you'll stand up to me, will you? Defend by attacking—you've got the harlot's answer all right. Do you know what I'm going to do? I'm going to throw you right into the water to drown, like the witch you are—"

"You dare!" She turned to the crowd. "You're all witnesses if he touches me. Look—he says I'm false because I've ventured to greet an old friend, and he's gone a-whoring all round the town with every creature in the taverns this twelvemonth past—ask him how many bastards in Bristol have his wicked face—"

They both stopped out of breath and stood panting at each other. A tall elderly man, one of Harry's friends, came forward, and put a hand on both their shoulders.

"Don't be fools, you two," he said. "Harry, I should say you've the worst of it. Go home and mend your ways, both of you. Here, Jane and Mary, you take Mistress Harry home, and Harry, you come and drink a can with me till you're in a better frame of mind."

The tension eased, the angry couple went off meekly with their respective escorts and the crowd broke up. Away out on the horizon, a ship went further and further away—and Gilbert wondered what had happened all those years to that pretty girl in the woodlands. He hadn't wanted to play her false, God was his witness. How could she have known that, that very night, the steward had come from Norfolk to fetch him home to his father's deathbed? And after that it had been too late. So she was gone, away over the horizon.

After Alison had cried herself to sleep in the big curtained bed, Harry came in, and woke her by stumbling over a stool—he was mellowed and chastened, both by the citizen's conversation and by his good wine. He poured out apologies—in the end he took her in his arms, and they resolved their conflict in lovers' fashion, and she slept.

But in the morning the bitter aftertaste was still there, and the hurt pride. Not only was he faithless to her, making her a byword to all the town, but now he'd be jealous as well, would he? And let all the town know it too. And she had rejected Thomas, and Jeremy, and tall Francis, and rich Master Benjamin, and God knows how many more, all for his sake.

He was jealous, was he? And what if she gave him grounds for jealousy? After all, who wouldn't? She knew without asking what Alison her godmother would have counselled: "No patient Grisell for you, my lass. Make him a cross of that same wood."

And—Gilbert was gone. That was a gratuitous blow. No good wondering, as she looked along the quay from her window, if one of those men might be Gilbert. Not for many months yet, if ever.

So—well . . .

Harry's ankle was well again, he decided within the week; and in another week he was off to sea again. And Alison bought herself a new gown and coif, and went out to wakes and carolling parties—where tall Francis found her suddenly less unapproachable.

When he came home from sea in October, she could tell the change in him. The years of hard drinking were beginning to show their effect—not just ale and wine, but Dutch strong waters and aquavitae. He first spent a few reasonably quiet nights with her at home, and was as affectionate and tender as ever, and kind to the boys; then, after a week, he was back at the tavern again.

He came home late, roaring to the skies. "Alison!" he yelled, as soon as he opened the door. "Alison, my lovely whore, are you there? Then take that—" and he hurled his heavy pewter tankard at her. His aim was bad and it went wide; and after a moment's astonishment she picked it up and flung it back at him. She did not throw to hit, but sent it past his ear, and it struck the door with a resounding bang.

"A broadside, by God!" he shouted, and laughed wildly. Then he collapsed on the floor, and passed out.

That was the beginning. After that, night after night, when he came home he threw things at her, pulled her about, wrestled with her, fought her—and she fought back. The first time that he took his big stick to her, she picked up the broom and defended herself as with a quarterstaff, and presently fetched him a crack on his head. He laughed heartily at that, rubbing his pate, and swore she could teach his master-at-arms a thing or two. After the first few occasions, she prudently put away her glass goblets, and her best pottery-ware, and everything that might be damaged. He didn't ask where they had gone—perhaps he thought they had broken them between them. The neighbours used to shake their heads at the noise, and vowed they could be heard from there to Plymouth.

It was a game at first—an uproarious rough game, at which she could always beat him, being sober. But it got a bit tiring, night after night, and after a while he was less playful and more malicious, and it grew less and less funny. It wasn't funny at all when he threatened the boys, not with his accustomed fatherly correction, but savagely—she withstood him, and protected them with animal fierceness, standing between him and the bed where they crouched, with her nails ready to claw him.

"God's bones, it's a bitch!" he said thickly, "a fighting bitch!"

"Yes!" she defied him. "True for you, I'm a

114

wolf-bitch, see? and if you lay a finger on the boys I'll have your eyes out."

After that he let the boys alone, but he fought her all round the house, night after night, till of the crockery-ware she left out for necessity, there wasn't a piece left whole. Wearily every morning, aching all over, she would have to set to and clear up the mess.

The neighbours were talking again—many men, especially in that seafaring community, got drunk now and again and beat their wives, but none so outrageously. Adam and Gamelyn shook their heads and said "It's the drink—," but none of them could try to stop him drinking. They marked how he began to sit about morosely during the day, his head in his hands, swigging now and then from his flask of aquavitae. His money was dwindling too. He made inroads on Alison's money (but she kept her little hidden hoard to herself)—and began soon to snatch things out of the house to sell or pawn—curtains, ornaments, Alison's jewels, her very gowns used to disappear. When the spring came round he made no move to go to sea again.

And then one night, as Alison sat waiting for his usual roaring return, she heard, instead, a hubbub and a shuffling of feet outside her door, and a crowd burst in, with Adam and Gamelyn in their midst, carrying Harry with the blood pouring out of a gash in his side. They laid him on the table, with his blood dripping down on the floor. He could not lift his head, but sought around with his eyes.

"Alison—oh, my poor Alison—are you there?"

She ran to him.

"Struck for death, I am. But I killed the bastard who

115

did it, so all's even. Alison, my love—oh, I've been a bad husband to you. A bad old bastard. I'm sorry.''

The tears were pouring down her face.

''No, dear love. Not a bad husband. A good husband—the best.''

And at that time she really meant it.

But when at last they covered his face, she drew a long sigh of relief, as if a violent storm had passed over her and was at length gone. She had peace at last—but how quiet and empty the house was now.

Yes, the storm was past, and she had escaped with her life; but oh, how empty, how silent. . . . When he had been away at sea before, it was different; one felt his lively personality somehow, ready to return sooner or later; but now—the empty chair to set against the wall, the quart tankard to hang up, the swaggering hat and thigh-boots to put away—and a silence that his loud voice would never break—

Oh, she had to have company in the long nights, if only to drive his ghost away from her pillow.

SIX

Fourth Husband

THERE were many to choose from—she might have had this one and that one and 'tother one—the young poet, for one, the sweet-voiced lad who was always rhyming of her. (What was his name? She could hardly remember.)

> Betwene March and Averil
> When spray ginneth to spring,
> The smalle fowles have their will
> In their own tongue to sing.
>
> I live in love-longing
> For seemliest of aller thing—
> She may me blisse bring—
> I am in her bandoun . . .

There had been some sweet nights—ah, and some

117

sweet stolen days. But none of them had counted for much—they were neither Harry nor Gilbert. But they kept her from loneliness in the tormenting nights:

> Night-times, when I toss and wake,
> Wherefore my cheeks be waxen wan . . .

But she would have to marry again. Which one to choose? She might no doubt have had the young poet, but he was a bird not to be caged. So with many of them. She considered them all—some marriageable, some not. Plenty of marriageable ones liked the look of her money even better than of her, for even Harry's extravagance had not left her as badly off as she feared, and her loom had now built her a steady trade which she worked at and increased, till she had three weavers under her and as useful a business as any in Bristol. So plenty of men, young and old, would have caught her for a prize; but the poet alone had not been one of them. Perhaps, she thought, he had run away from her lest he should be thought to covet her money. A pity, poor Philip—yes, that was the name. Poor sweet Philip.

Plenty of others had taken up the song after he had left her:

> Of hue her hair is fair enow—
> Her browé brown, her eyé black—
> She looks on me with lovesome brow,
> Her middle's small and well y-made.
> But she will me to her take
> Her own sweetheart for to make,
> Longer to live I shall forsake
> And feyé fall a-down.

Whether or no, she would consider very carefully now what she did. Harry had been a wonderful experience, and she would not have forgone him; but no man should tyrannize her now, riot in her house, waste her goods, beat her, make her ashamed before the neighbours. Harry had begun by being a genial fire to warm her heart; in the end he was a conflagration that threatened to burn up house and all. No more of such. Moreover, she had learnt now to have her cake and eat it—a night of love, an afternoon or so in a garden or an evening under the moon, and then— goodbye, my sweet, 'tis safer so. No tie, no obligation, none of the demands of marriage—

Why, then, get married at all? Oh, the world demanded it. A woman could not live by herself. They all plagued her and drove her this way and that, pressing to know *whom* she would marry, this rich eligible young widow—for appearance's sake, and for peace, she must take a husband. She could not play Penelope with her web forever. And so in the end she took meek old Baldwin, and on the strength of all she had learnt, tamed him to her wish.

Poor man! She often laughed, in after years, when she thought of what she had made him go through. He had been a bachelor, though quite fifty by that time, and knew very little about women; and Alison kept him in a constant state of surprise. He, with his inexperience, came in for the full benefit of her experience; and he was soon a model of astonished submission. Some hidden streak of cruelty must have been waked up in Alison by Harry's disappointment of her; and she had to work it off on poor Baldwin. She defended herself by attacking—accusing him of every fault, from that of coveting her money to carnal intentions towards her maids. And in the end, having subdued and moulded him to her own desire, she discovered that she loathed and despised him.

It was at this point that the long-suffering man had an inspiration.

"Alison, love," he said one bright spring morning, after her tongue had kept him awake all night, "why don't you go on a pilgrimage?"

She stopped as she was picking up a dish from the table, and set it down again. Her heart gave a wild jump, but she held her head scornfully. "Pilgrimage, by'r Lady? What's got into you, husband? Me go on a pilgrimage?"

"Yes, love, why not? You could go to Walsingham or to Canterbury, or to—to—to"—he tried to think of some place sufficiently far away.

"To—to—to! You hoot like an old owl. Why not to Compostella—why not to Rome—to Jerusalem—to the moon, indeed?"

"I hardly think you'd get *there,*" he said, with his sober humourless smile. "But some palmers go all the way to Jerusalem even, and come back with cockleshells and palms, and Jordan holy water—"

She spun about on her heel and laughed loudly.

"Oho, good man, you're in a hurry to pack me off! You want me out of the way, I'll wager. Oh yes, so that as soon as my back's turned you can revel it with Kate and Dorothy—*I* know, you lurking old lozel. Send me on a pilgrimage! That's a fine idea—to pray for your dusty old soul and all its sins—fie, fie, go and do your own praying in the church. I'll not fetch one cockleshell from Saint Jiminy for you. Go on a pilgrimage indeed!"

"Why, Alison, you'd love it. It would do your health good, sweetheart, indeed it would. Your lads be all grown up and 'prenticed now, and no more care to you. I'll mind the house for you. You shall have money to spare—"

"I should think so too, seeing it's all mine. Why, look—I haven't a robe fit to go as far as Exeter in, let alone a pilgrimage—so niggardly you keep me—"

"You shall have all you want. Come, there was my cousin's gossip went to Rome last year and was blessed by the Holy Father himself—she joined herself to a company of decent gentlefolks, and lodged at pilgrims' inns along the way—and saw all the wonders of the world—Naples, and Venice—"

Venice! A flash of colour and gorgeousness, a breath of warmth and perfume—brocades, ambers—peacocks, apes and ivory. . . . But Alison gave no sign, but went on resisting, mocking, pouring scorn on the idea, by degrees letting old Baldwin thrust upon her, as if sore against her will, her very heart's desire. (And hadn't she done the same this time? she pondered, when young Gilbert and his wife had persuaded her to go to Canterbury . . .)

In the end, "Well, well, sweetheart—go I will, to please you."

"Thank God!" breathed the old man, picking up a candlestick and toddling off with it. "I mean—thank God for the good it will do thy health, sweetheart."

And so she came to set out overseas—round the world, as it was known then, and right on to its centre, Jerusalem. Further by a long way than Adam, Gamelyn or even Harry. She had already outdone her brothers in money-making.

Pilgrimages were hardly as difficult in those days as one might suppose. Being both fashionable and pious, they had the approbation of both earth and heaven; the intention was religious, whatever elements might creep in later; and they were very good for trade. So, all over the known world, bands of holy hikers travelled to surprising distances, and the power of the Church protected, encouraged, and organized them right across Europe, well into Asia, and back again.

Every monastery offered the pilgrims a lodging; religious and chivalric orders stood by to protect them; and robbers were seldom so hardy as to offer them any annoyance—indeed, it paid better to exploit them peacefully, like succeeding ages. Parties of pilgrims were usually large and mixed, and well able to take care of each other; some companies would stick together faithfully for a whole journey, but many pilgrims would skip from party to party at the main ports, as they found company that suited them best. Alison was, naturally, one of these.

Equipment was of a practical kind; the "cockle hat and staff and sandal shoon" were no picturesque trimmings, but necessary items—the broad-brimmed felt hat for shade, sometimes turned up like a bush hat, with a cockleshell stuck at the side or front if one had *really* been to Compostella, and a few additional ones for further journeys—and as much opportunity for line-shooting as, nowadays, hotel labels on suitcases. The staff and sandals were for easy walking—but the wise pilgrim added a pair of riding boots as well, and rode a horse, a donkey, a mule or what he could get, whenever possible—Alison even rode a camel a time or two. The hodden-grey cape and hood was useful against rain and dust. A small pack would carry a very minimal change of linen, and a snack for the day; but again, the wily ones even when walking took care to have a pack-animal for their belongings. A pilgrim's real wealth, however—money, and for the sake of compact value, precious stones—travelled as close to his skin as possible—no other way was safe. It made things easier if you had business connections among the merchants of the big cities, for even at this time, letters of credit were used; and Alison did not, therefore, have to carry too much money on her, since Harry and her brothers had long ago made contacts even as far away as Venice.

SEVEN

First Pilgrimage

SO away she went, and who shall describe the days of wonder that followed? To London first, then to Calais and on to Paris; westward to the Pyrenees and into Spain; round the coast, down Italy; across to Naples, and to great Rome itself; away up to Venice, down the Adriatic by ship, to Malta, Cyprus, Rhodes and at last to Joppa and the Holy Land . . . and Jerusalem. The Holy City, the Holy Sepulchre—and what other place on earth should a Christian seek?

There had been an old man in the company, a very old man who had died when he reached the Holy Sepulchre. Just knelt down, lifted up his hands and eyes, and died.

Two full years she travelled about Europe and the East. Oh, she had seen the world—she had tasted it and rolled it on her tongue, and whenever it might please God to call her, she'd thank Him for the life she'd had. She would remember so many things—perils and hardships, true, weariness and fasting and the malice of the sea—the awful snows of Switzerland, when they had nearly died on that high pass—but how merry they had been round the fires in the monastery afterwards! But most of all she would remember the gaiety, the colour, the life—Spain, with its vivid darkness and brightness, its sharp cold air, its hot scorching days and star-pierced nights—Italy, all luscious and flowery—Palestine, fantastic and holy, like an old mass-book come alive.

Strange things had happened to her. At Constantinople they had met with the smallpox, and she was terrified. Dying she could face like a Christian, but to be disfigured, to become hideous, she could not bear that. She confided her fear to Ahmed, who was very fond of her, and a dear fellow though a heathen Mussulman. He took her out of the city at night, away into the mountains, to a stone-built house, bare but clean, and introduced her to an old crone who was his mother. This old crone said prayers and spells over Alison and did all manner of heathen things, and then scratched Alison's arm with the point of a knife and rubbed something in. She then made Alison go to bed; and when Alison woke, she was in a raging fever, and the smallpox had hold of her; soon her arm was blistered all over and burnt as if in hell fire; but the sores never touched her face. The old woman sat by her bedside, bathed and sponged her and recited more spells; and when the days and nights ran into a fiery blur, and the devils gnawed Alison's arm, she sometimes felt the old woman holding her with incredible strength, restraining her so that she could not scratch the arm—though Alison shrieked aloud for a surgeon to cut it off. And then she seemed to sleep, and woke cool and relaxed though deathly weak, and knew that the sickness had burnt itself out and she was alive. Her arm was scarred in a dozen places with deep pits, but nowhere else on her body had the plague set its mark—above all, her face was untouched. Ahmed told her that now she was quit of the smallpox for ever, and could walk through a city full of it and take no harm. And he kissed her lovingly—and then as she had grown stronger and thrived on mountain milk and honey, how he had coaxed the pleasure back into her limbs, and praised his Allah for her smooth cheeks whenever he laid his own against them. . . .

So she had spent the winter in the mountains above Constantinople, and in the spring she had gone again to Jerusalem. It was hard to leave Ahmed, but after all, he was a heathen Mussulman, and she was a Christian and must go to Jerusalem by Easter. All over Palestine the red anemones bloomed—and the ignorant heathen said that they were the blood of the god Tammuz, whereas every good Christian knew they commemorated the Blood of the Lord.

And then at last, knowing that all things must come to an end—and especially money—she had returned home. Baldwin was glad to see her, poor old fellow, and so were her boys. Gilbert was a grown man over twenty-three, and the others were seventeen, fifteen, and thirteen, and terrorizing the town. They were all apprenticed, even the youngest, who went along with his next brother; for they were far too precocious and mischievous to keep in any Christian man's house, and they had nearly killed poor Baldwin between them till Alison sent them away into apprenticeship before her departure. Now she came back, and took up the reins of her household, and tried to settle down as best she might—but heigh-ho, how dull it was.

EIGHT
Maying in Bath

NOW dull—she could find nothing to satisfy her energies but to tease and torment Baldwin, and put on the act of the capricious woman, always wanting what she hadn't got, and harrying him half out of his mind. Her cunning fancy was to go back to Bath and settle there once more; and of course Baldwin had to yield to her. She had several reasons for this, but of course told him none of them—one was that her godsib Alison Barton, now a widow, had come to live in Bath. Another reason was that she longed to flaunt herself before her old neighbours, now that she was older and bolder—yes, and richer too. For her fortune had not declined while she went about Europe; she had left Baldwin as steward over her looms, and he had managed them well enough. He was a retired linen-draper and knew something of cloth and weaving; and having given up his trade, he was restless with nothing to do, and rejoiced to be given charge of Alison's business, to poke and peer and cheese-pare and cast up accounts. The wool trade was just beginning its spectacular rise; Alison had brought back some fresh techniques from Flanders, France, and Italy as she passed through; and in Bath there would be less competition than in Bristol. So the looms clacked away, and what Alison had spent on her travels was soon recouped.

So Alison's return to Bath was as impressive as her departure had been scandalous. She was rich enough now to be admired and courted by all the snobs in the town, and if the old slanders were remembered at all, they were overlaid by the prestige of her money. Alison often laughed to herself, cynically, over this. Her stepdaughters, now ageing and depressed, moped in their old-fashioned seclusion—Lucas's house, that they had been so genteel about, was far outshone now by Alison's new one; and on Sundays Alison would sweep past them down the church, in the most mountainous coif ever seen, to present her church-offering the first of all the congregation. Those smug old women who had once crowed over her and browbeat her so—now it was her turn to crow over them, and she made the most of it.

The meeting with Alison Barton was a joyous and tearful occasion. There was so much to say—the first time they had talked all night, and for long, long after that there were treasures to be fetched up from the dusty boxes of memory. Alison Barton was over sixty, but very hale and comely. Wat had left her enough, when all was sold, to buy a little cottage in the town—she could not manage the farm without him, nor could she bear the loneliness. So she helped out her little store by letting lodgings to a young man.

He had looked out of the window at Alison standing below—he lounged there in the window, idly, laughing—he had whistled to her as if she had been a young girl, and all of a sudden she *was* a young girl again. His hair was yellow and hung down to his shoulders; his skin was delicate rose and white, like a girl's, but there was nothing meek or milksop in his looks—bold twinkling blue eyes, a cynical mouth, eyebrows that danced, and a swaggering, lounging gesture whether he stood or sat. He wore the outrageous new dress of the times—long hose most indecently skin-tight, with a codpiece, all divided into halves of red and white (as if, old Baldwin said one day, he had been flayed of one side).

"Who's that young man?" she asked Alison Barton, as soon as she was within doors.

"Him? Oh, he's my lodger. Jenkyn, the clerk at the wine-merchant's. Here, Jenkyn, come down, you slothful sluggard, and meet a fair lady."

Jenkyn came down the loft steps flourishing his slim legs. He and Alison stood looking at one another; and then he took her hand with a gesture that took possession of her, saying simply, "My dear!"

From that moment her heart was his.

So time and opportunity came about. . . .

Alison Barton, in spite of her years, was a great organizer of parties. Picnics, we would call them—the idea is far older than the name. She would gather a gang of young people—and some not so young, but all gay and ready for pleasure; and off they would go, with their baskets of cakes and flagons of ale, along the river banks or into the greenwood. Lords and ladies went hunting, with servants to carry their baked meats and wine; but the townsfolk dispensed with the servants and the ceremony, and went "a-Maying," even if it were June, July or August. They made themselves green garlands and crowned one another; they sang rounds and catches; if they went by the level meads along the river, they danced or played kissing games; sometimes on very hot days they would bathe, and nobody thought of bathing-costumes. You could only do these lovely things in the summer, and summer was so short.

It was on a lovely day in May—as always, Alison's fateful month—when Alison Barton had gathered one of these parties, and our Alison walked side by side with Jenkyn. What a day! How sweet with leaves, how blue with bluebells—they walked along garlanded with flowers, great moist luscious collars and crowns of bluebells and cowslips—it was so hot, she had slipped her gown off her shoulders, and it hung from her waist, and she hid her breasts only with that thick garland of flowers . . . they were walking slowly, far behind the rest, and no one could see them. Somewhere ahead, another young man in the party thrummed a lute, and two or three voices sang, softly, lazily.

"It's almost like Italy," she sighed.

He laughed at her.

"Italy, Italy! You're a spoilt madam. This is good enough for me. Isn't it for you?"

They stopped and the music went further away from them.

"I'll bet people don't walk as fast as this in Italy," he went on. "I'm tired—here, sit down."

That was just his imperious, petulant way. She knew it by this time. She sat down. What did he say to her after that? Oh, how could she remember? What mattered was that her middle age was suddenly youth—that he was as ardent a lover to her as if she had been a girl of his own age—that she blossomed under his caresses as a tree blossoms again after the winter.

"Alison—if you were free—supposing old Baldwin died—"

"Baldwin isn't dead—you mustn't say such things."

"No, but he's old. He's older than Mistress Barton. Anything might befall him—"

"Ah, but I'm old too." She leaned back, conscious of her beauty, and mocked him.

"Old? You're *not* old! You are like Aurora, who was made young with every dawn, and your poor old Baldwin is Tithonus, whom she made immortal but forgot to make young." For Jenkyn always had a very pretty taste in learned allusions. "No, but if he did die, Alison my lovely, would you marry me?"

"Do you mean it, Jenkyn? You so young, and I—nearly forty?" (Oh yes, she was forty-four and over.)

"I wouldn't care if you were fifty. I mean it, my dear. I swear it. Tell me—"

"Well—" Even then, she looked ahead, weighed, and considered. She pondered to herself: what I say now can bind me but little, for Baldwin's not dead. But a mouse must have more than one hole to run into from the cat! One should keep a reserve handy—and such a reserve! Too young—and can I trust him? Pooh, I can take care of myself, and—he's so lovely! Aloud she said,

"Well, wait till the time comes. . . ." The rest was obliterated in caresses.

They walked back, all together, through the serene evening, too serene to last. Strolling easily along the smooth green meadow, light garments flying, lutes thrumming, garlands transforming them into a festival pageant; the level sun behind them making the river banks, the trees, the hedges, a richer and glassier green, and the town as they neared it all of coral and ivory. And Alison leaned on Jenkyn's arm and sang.

Then, as they passed through the town gates, and neared Alison Barton's house, an old woman in dismal dark clothes, one of Baldwin's servants, came running out to meet them, and suddenly Alison thought of the day when Joan had come hammering and shouting below the weaving-loft—

"Oh, my God, Agnes, what is it?"

"Master Baldwin, mistress—it's the smallpox. There's three or four more taken with it, and now we're all going to die, oh Lord! oh Lord! oh Lord!" And the woman went off into a high-pitched shriek, and threw the apron over her head.

The party checked and wavered.

"Oh God—the smallpox!"

The terror went through them like a wave. Without a word of farewell most of them turned and went their several ways. Alison Barton and Jenkyn remained standing, looking at each other.

"What's to do now?" said Alison Barton.

Alison pressed her lips together, as one making a decision. She pushed the garland back, and showed her left arm.

"Look—the pest can't touch me. I've had my share,

133

and I'm a safe woman now. I'll stay and nurse poor Baldwin."

"I'll stay with you then," said her godsib. "I'm old and I've had my life. God forbid I should leave you in your need."

Alison turned to Jenkyn. "And you, Jenkyn?" He was pale, and his blue eyes were big.

"Do—do you want me to stay by you, sweetheart?"

She could see so plainly that he was terrified lest she should ask him to stay.

"No, no, Jenkyn. Run away for your life. Go anywhere, and keep away till I send word to you. The—the mouse may need another hole."

"I—I thank you. You—know I—would have stayed, had you bidden me?"

"I know." She suppressed a smile. Poor Jenkyn—much he would!

"Look!" He drew aside from the other Alison. "Will you put my ring on your finger—be plighted to me if he dies?"

"God forbid! He's not dead yet—I dare not think of it—Oh, Jenkyn, don't let such a wicked thought cross your mind! I must pray for him to live—I must do all I can to save him. You too must pray that he may be spared—"

"Of course, of course." They nodded gravely to each other—kissed, as the fashion of the time allowed, and oh, how her heart leapt at the touch of his fresh smooth cheek!—shook hands, and so parted. Once out of sight of her, he ran at top speed to Alison Barton's house, snatched his books, his money and his clothes, flung down payment for his lodging, and fled out of the town without stopping to draw breath.

While Alison Barton, her arm round her godchild's waist, went on into the stricken house.

And through the dark, hot, fetid nights that followed, how Alison tried to govern her thoughts and her prayers as she sat by Baldwin's bed! It was true, as Ahmed had foretold—no infection could lay hold upon Alison, and though weary, faint and overwatched, she remained well, when all were stricken around her. All her boys were far enough away—she sent no word to them, though by this time she could have made shift to write a sort of a letter; but even a word-of-mouth messenger, she knew, might carry the sickness in his clothes. So she contented herself with knowing that they were out of reach. But after ten days Alison Barton took the smallpox, and before the week was out Alison had closed her dear godsib's eyes and stood by her grave, in a field of so many, many graves. She walked home under the shadow of death, to the dark house where old Agnes, herself now just able to walk, recovering from the sickness but blind in one eye, kept such watch as she could over Baldwin, who was rapidly sinking after a brief rally. People had looked after Alison walking through the streets, unscathed and vigorous—had the old whisper of "witchcraft" gone round again?

She sat by the deathbed, sunk in misery. Much good it was to her now, to be whole and sound in the midst of death! Was God angry with her, because her thoughts had strayed to Jenkyn, that He had taken away her only true friend? Oh, but she had done her best for Baldwin—she had nursed him dutifully, devotedly, as best she knew. She had kept those bungling physicians away from him, too. She had tried all her grandmother's herbal skill on him, which was far better than the doctor's—and so she had on her godsib. Yes, but hadn't she wanted Baldwin to die, wicked woman that she was? And had her sinful wish stricken down her friend too? No, no—she hadn't wanted him to die. He—he wasn't dead yet—he might live—please God, let him live. . . .

He was dead.

And so she followed the gloomy procession to the churchyard. The plague was abating now, and a proper number of neighbours could be mustered to give Baldwin a decent funeral, with six young men to carry his coffin. Six young men—and as she walked behind, her black veil over her face, not lifting her eyes, she could just see their legs—a fine pair of legs the one at the back had. Like Jenkyn's. . . . At the thought, so mixed were her feelings that something between a giggle and a sob caught her at the back of the throat. She stuffed her handkerchief into her mouth, and the tears gushed from her eyes. She leant hard on the arm of the kind neighbour who walked with her.

"Aren't you feeling well, love?" said the neighbour.

"It's nothing—take no notice," said Alison.

NINE

The Gallows Bird

AND so the winter came again, and when another spring cleansed the world, and every house in Bath had burned its pest-infected beds and curtains, and the town felt safe again, one day there was a knock at Alison's door, and "Are you glad to see me?" said Jenkyn.

"Glad? You are the spring and the blessed sunshine," she replied. And from thence on he was her guest.

How merry they were together, those days! He had such a sparkling wit, he was so mocking and teasing, and yet so loving—day after day passed happily, but now he never spoke to her of marriage. After a long time, using the privilege and boldness of an older woman, she spoke to him, and reminded him of his promise; he was very affectionate, very loving and passionate to her, but said it was too soon yet—she must surely wait till her husband had been dead a year?—and then he had business to see to, and so on, and so on. The merchant whom he had previously served had another clerk, and how Jenkyn lived she had no idea, but he seemed to have money of his own. He took lodgings in her house and paid her fairly for his board; other widows took lodgers, why shouldn't she? He had the run of the house, and made himself very much at home.

She usually worked in her workshop with her assistants from breakfast time to noon; he occupied himself in the town, taking on casual jobs, he said, such as "scriveyne" to parsons, lawyers and other learned men; and about noon, old Agnes would serve them both their dinner. But one day (as she remembered so clearly) she came in and waited dinner for him, and he was not there; nor for a full hour after she had dined. Agnes had not seen him since breakfast. Oh well, men would be late for dinner. Then as it happened, she needed a gold piece to pay the carter for bringing some yarn. Her wealth was now in the cloth bales in her warehouse and the gold and silver vessels that the goldsmith kept for her, but she still kept a bag of gold pieces in the coffer behind the loose panel. She opened the panel and put her hand out for the coffer. It closed on emptiness.

Suddenly cold with shock, she ran round the house. To the place where her silver candlesticks had stood—they stood no longer. To her jewel box—not a brooch nor a chain remained to her. To Jenkyn's room—it was all too plain. His clothes and books were gone, and his lute—gone in haste, the cupboard doors left swinging open, bedclothes tossed about, curtains disordered, as if in contempt—

138

She sat down suddenly, feeling faint. Gone, all gone. Oh, what a fool she had been, what a fool, what a green, trusting, childish fool! and he—he'd mocked her, taken advantage of her, as a silly, credulous old woman. Doubtless he thought she would be ashamed to seek justice against him—or too soft-hearted and forgiving. If he thought so, he should think again. The swine!

She sprang to her feet, and rushed out of the house, yelling and shrieking. "Whoa—justice, justice—I'm robbed, I'm robbed, I'm robbed." Dignity and grace thrown to the winds—red-faced, sweating, uncoiffed, her tawny hair flying in streels, her mouth wide stretched—bellowing and running through the streets—gathering the crowd round her like a swarming queen-bee, and crying for vengeance like all Bedlam together, till she sank to the ground sobbing.

The men caught him up half way between Bath and Bristol, with the loot still on him and no need for further evidence. He offered no violence—he wasn't that sort of thief. He only wept and prayed for mercy, both then and before the magistrate afterwards. Alison looked him in the face quite pitilessly, and heard him sentenced to be hanged.

To be hanged by the neck till he was dead. And serve him right—and of course, may the Lord have mercy on his soul. His black, tricky soul—the poor devil. Alison walked home very slowly from the courthouse, avoiding her sympathetic neighbours. She had all her belongings back, and they would hang him tomorrow. Tonight they would send a priest to him to make his shrift, tomorrow early he would receive the last rites, and then, of course, he would be hanged as thieves always were. The townsfolk would enjoy the sight. Alison herself had seen quite a number of very interesting hangings at one time and another, as well as some fancy executions in Spain, Palestine and Constantinople. It was her right, of course, to be a principal spectator at this one—but somehow she felt it wouldn't be enjoyable at all. No, she wouldn't see him hanged. Poor wretch—but even if she stayed at home tomorrow, she would pass the gallows every time she went outside the town gates, and would see his fine young body dangling there until it became unrecognizable. She hadn't minded seeing those two sheep-stealers there all last winter—why should she mind Jenkyn? But no, argue it how she would, she could not bear the thought. All night she sat by her fireside and turned it over in her mind. She remembered the living man, so soon to be the unsightly corpse swinging at the gate—merry young Jenkyn, with his sweet voice and his blue eyes, his ready wit and his strong arms—he was her love, her own, her well-beloved—all his precious youth and beauty that had once been her own. . . .

And should be her own now. The first streak of dawn was in the sky, and a bell had begun to toll. Suddenly resolved, Alison rose from beside her fire, dressed and coiffed herself with deliberate care; and while the bell still tolled, set forth into the streets. A crowd was gathering, as always, for the hanging; she walked resolutely through them, right to the place, and waited there. There was no scaffold, only the tall gallows-tree outside the town gate, with the cleared space below to which a cart would be driven, and afterwards driven away again. . . . She watched the hangman climb over the crossbeam and attach a new rope with a carefully made noose. Shouts from the crowd told that the cart was approaching.

It came up rumbling and jolting—a high structure, built to give a good drop; Jenkyn placed high on it, with the priest and the hangman's assistant by his side. His arms were bound, and the wind fanned his fair hair—he looked terribly handsome, and so young.

The cart reached the gallows' foot.

It was then that Alison stepped boldly forward, and said in a voice that was heard right across the crowd:

"I claim this man as my promised husband."

The crowd gasped, and then buzzed with excited talk. Yes, that was the law—a woman might do it. Any felon could be reprieved from death if a woman would claim him at the gallows' foot as her affianced husband. It had not been done for years, but it was still the law. And quite right too—there was poor Mary Whiting, that the old folks remembered—her man, robber though he was, had been reprieved by her, she being five months gone with child—or else how could she have been honestly married and her poor brat provided for? Yes, it was the law—

And Alison came forward, bold and firm, as they all stood doubting, and repeated what she had said. The hangman stood still with the noose in his hand, and the constable ran to fetch Master Wickham, the magistrate, who was still in bed. His Worship came running and panting, huddling on his gown as he came, and his wife came running too, relishing a first-rate scandal.

"What's this, what's this, what's this?" cried His Worship.

"Yes, Your Worship, hear me. This is I, Alison Baldwin, widow of this town, and I claim this man,

Jenkyn Johnson, clerk, as my affianced husband.''

Master Wickham cleared his throat, and settled the collar of his gown.

"Jenkyn Johnson, clerk, is this true? Are you troth-plight to this woman, and willing to be her lawful wedded husband, and bound to be of good behaviour, if your life is spared?''

"Oh, yes, yes!'' Poor Jenkyn's eyes were starting from his head, and the red and white chased each other across his face—two great tears tolled down his cheeks, and his pinioned hands could not wipe them away.

"Be it so.'' Master Wickham nodded curtly to the hangman. "You're bail for his life and answerable for his good conduct, mistress. Let him go.''

A cheer rose from the crowd, as the hangman's mate cut Jenkyn's bonds. Only a few of the town's matrons whispered and muttered. Oh yes, Alison knew she had done for her good name now forever.

Jenkyn ran forward and cast himself at her feet, blubbering, embracing her knees, kissing her hands, calling her saviour; angel, Madonna, mother of mercies. She lifted him up to her as one lifts a child, and pressed her lips to his brow—fresh and alive and saved from ugly death! And gathering him into her arms with loving tenderness, led him home to her house in joy and love.

TEN

Fifth Husband

SO began for Alison a life of mingled pleasure and pain—between roses and swords, and never a dull moment anyway. She knew that Jenkyn would be a difficult proposition, but she was wise to him now, and knew what to expect. To do him justice, he never again attempted crime—he had been too thoroughly frightened, and Alison now had the upper hand of him—another slip, he knew, would be his last. Also he was, in his irresponsible way, very fond of her. In spite of their disparity of age, they each found the other a satisfying lover; there was that about Alison that would attract and satisfy any man, and in spite of her forty-odd years, she could inspire more passion in Jenkyn than any number of green young maidens; and she for her part met his love-making with all that frank enjoyment that Harry had so admired. Jenkyn was, of course, a rover by nature, and by no means faithful; but she knew better than to be jealous now, and he was more circumspect than Harry, and knew better than to provoke her to jealousy; and always, after his wanderings, he would come back to her with: "You're worth a thousand of them."

That was the sweet side—but the other—well, she had known how it would be. Of course he was a spendthrift and a waster, and lived entirely on Alison, but she had expected that. She kept him on an allowance, and locked everything away that he might have laid hands on. An expensive pet, was he? Well—other women had their dogs and squirrels and marmots—and how many rich old men spent their wealth on pretty young mistresses? Her sons were well provided for, and she took care to deposit money and jewels with her brothers for safe keeping. How angry he used to get when she wouldn't allow him more—yes, he'd the devil's temper, and oh how he'd fight, yes, and claw and bite and scratch and throw the furniture about. One night loving caresses, and the next night beating—that was the pattern. But it didn't frighten her—what! She'd lived with Harry, and this was a cock-sparrow's temper to a lion's. She could fight back too and did. What times they did have, and how they smashed up chairs and mirrors and glasses, and then fell into each other's arms embracing. . ...

She could have borne everything but his sarcastic tongue.

He was at a disadvantage, and knew it; and his only outlet was that which custom allots to the woman—the victory of words. He used his cleverness to humiliate her, and so compensate himself for having sold himself into her hands. He knew how helpless he was, and his resentment turned to an underrunning jealousy, which expressed itself in sly, sophisticated ways that drove Alison wild.

He had a book, a great heavy brown volume—printed, too, which was a costly rarity, and illustrated with engravings. If it had been English she could have spelled out a few words of it—the titles under the pictures at least, and the chapter-headings—but it was all in Latin, every blessed word, and she couldn't understand it at all. He would sit in the chimney corner, to get a good blaze from the fire, and chuckle and chuckle to himself over it, as if it had been a fine chapbook of bawdy jests, and hum and ha, and nod his head as if agreeing—

"For the Lord's sake," she said to him, "what's that book called?"

He looked up at her with a smirk.

"It's called *Epistola Valerii and Rufinum de ne ducenda uxorem*—"

"Eh, what? Epistle-ah-Valeri-ee—what's that in a Christian man's tongue?"

"Letter from Valerius to Rufinus, see you, advising him not to get married."

"Oh indeed!" She tossed her head. "And what reasons does Master Valerius give?"

"Plenty." He ran the pages under his thumb—they were thick, solid, crackling pages. "Look at all these women. Every one of them was a wicked wife: here's Samson and his Delilah—she cut his hair off with her shears—and there's Dejaneira, that gave Hercules a fiery shirt, that burnt him to death—there's Socrates—look at his horrid shrewish Xanthippe—do you see what she's pouring on his head, poor man? Oh, how well I sympathize with him!" And he gave a heartrending sigh.

"Go on with you, saucy," she said, "or I'll give you Xanthippe!" And she laughed, but somehow she did not laugh it off. The idea stuck, and rankled. And just when she had put it out of her mind, he would start it up again.

"Where are you going this evening, Alison, all dressed up in your best? Do you know, you wear your best clothes every day of the week?"

"Yes, it keeps the moths out of them. I'm going dancing, if you want to know—across at Bessie's."

"Going dancing? You gad about too much! You're married to me now."

"Oh, am I so? And so I'm to sit at home, am I? Who says so?"

"There was a man in Rome, so this book says," and he tapped the cover solemnly, "who cast his wife off because she went out to a summer party without his leave. . . . Yes, and look at this one—Simplicius Gallus—he saw his wife looking out of the window bare-headed, and he cast her off too. And here's wise Solomon, who said that a foolish woman, who goeth from house to house, is like—"

"Ha! And you'll quote your Solomon at me, will you? Plague take you and your book." And out of doors she went, her head held high.

Blast the man, young enough to be her son and taking the high hand of her like that—ordering her about and reproving her. She told him one day she wanted to go on another pilgrimage. The obstinate look came into his eye again.

"You know what they say:

Whoso buildeth his house of sallows.

And pricketh his blind horse over the fallows,
And suffereth his wife to go seeking hallows,
Is—

And then he remembered the last line, reddened, and dried up. She finished it for him, laughing loud and coarsely:

"Is worthy to be hanged on the gallows!"

"Oh, you cursed woman!" he flared up. "You get a man in your toils, and he's your bondslave—"

He sat down again with a controlled, self-martyring smile. He knew his deadliest form of attack.

"But I say nothing. No, I sit by and read my book, and commune with the philosophers—Jerome and Tertullian, Solomon and Ovid—Socrates too, though you were crueller than Xanthippe—I'll read about Livia who poisoned Drusus, and Lucia who slew her husband with a love-potion, and so on and so on. . . ." He plunged his head down over the big volume, and folded the leaves up almost to his ears, and hummed and mummed away to himself, while she stood there chafing.

So I'm to go to no more parties, am I? And no more pilgrimages—the proud little pimp—

But that night he took her in his arms and was all honey and fire, and she adored him and swore she could not live without him.

Till at last there came that evening she so well remembered.

He had gone through and through his book, over and over, and told her every story till she knew them by heart, and every one pointed at her—and all his proverbs and saws too, about wanton women and contentious wives—like dripping eaves, like a gold ring in a sow's nose—better to abide on the rooftop, etc. etc. etc.

And there he was in the firelight, mumbling and gloating—this time it was over the picture of that horrible unnatural Pasiphaë, Queen of Crete, with the bull—Lord! it made one sick to think of it. . . .

"Oh, put that book away for God's sake," she said.

"Not I. It's a rare book. Come now, let me read you some—here's Clytemnestra, who killed her husband with an axe, for her paramour's sake. Here's the picture. As I live, she has a look of you."

"Stop it, Jenkyn!"

"And here's one that drove a nail through a man's head while he slept—ah, and here's wicked Eve herself, the downfall of all the human race—"

"You and your Eve—and what of Adam, then?"

"Adam was the man God made, to keep her in order, but she ruined him and all men after him. Look, here's Hypsipile, and Trotula, and Euphile. . . ."

She couldn't bear any more.

"You and your Hipsi-pipsi-lee!" she screamed out—a great wave of anger burst in her and she snatched the book out of his hands, grabbed a handful of pages out of the middle, and tore with all her might—

Up he sprang to his feet—"My book! You traitress, my book!"

He struggled with her—she lashed out with one hand, still clutching the book with the other, and sent him staggering back into the fire. He sat down on the hot coals, and sprang up again with a yelp—a smell of singeing filled the air—disregarding it, he closed with her, wrenched the book from her grasp, and swung the heavy volume against the side of her head—it smote her like a thunderbolt.

She went down into blackness and silence.

When she opened her eyes, she saw his face swimmingly and blurred above her; her head was buzzing and ringing like a belfry, like a beehive—her ears felt a strange unevenness, too, as if one side of her head was heavier than the other. Jenkyn's voice came to her, faint and muffled.

"Oh, Alison, Alison, dear sweetheart!—Oh God, I've killed her!"

Faint as she was, there was a cunning instinct that even then told Alison the right move to make. She closed her eyes again and lay back.

"You've killed me, Jenkyn. My money, was it? . . . You'll have it all, now . . . Yes, you've killed me . . . but . . . let me . . . kiss you . . . once . . ."

He was weeping now, holding her against her breast.

"Oh, my love, my love, forgive me! Oh, don't die, Alison . . . oh, as God's my witness, I'll never lay hand on you again—oh, Alison, Alison—"

She gave him a pathetic smile as he bent over to kiss her.

"Farewell, false love—" and then she fainted away in good earnest.

But as she swooned, her teeth met in the lobe of his ear, making him yelp like a puppy. Whether this was spite, ecstasy or a convulsion, he never knew—nor indeed did she.

She came to, presently, laid on her bed, vinegar bandages on her head, her maid and a dozen friends fussing round her, and Jenkyn sobbing at the bed's foot. And from that day on he was her slave. There was nothing he would not do for her. He gave her no more trouble—he came and went at her bidding, with dog-like devotion and submission. The fact was, the shadow of a second gallows had been more than he could bear. Old Baldwin himself had hardly been so submissive. And so she had everything she wanted, even to making him get rid of that book. But from the time she came out of thàt swoon, she was deaf in one ear ever after. She could hear, but only at half strength and from one side; and there were many qualities of tone that she missed.

And when she begged him to let her go to "the hallows" again to pray that her deafness might be cured, he had not a word to say against it.

So that she set off again cheerfully—and eventually found herself, one morning, sitting on the sands of Morocco, in deadly peril of having her head struck off by the Moors.

ELEVEN

The Moors and—Martyrdom?

NOT dry sunshine poured down upon the sands of Morocco, where Alison, shaded by her big felt hat with the cockleshell on it, sat on a pile of baggage and waited.

The light was such as she had never known in England, though by now it was not strange to her; blue sea, and yellow desert, brighter than the glass in any church window; hot white stones, and scarce a shadow of any other colour, save a mile away the orange- and palm-trees grouped around a flat-topped, walled house, and rather nearer, some splashes of red, brown, orange, black and white, where half a dozen Moors stood guard over Alison's companions. These were ten nuns of varying ages, from a pair of old tough superiors down to three round-eyed, fresh-faced postulants of seventeen, now clinging in a bunch about the knees of the older ones, and all weeping and perspiring together. On a sandbank some way out in the water could be seen the up-ended timbers of the little ship that had brought them on this unlucky stage of their journey; and on the sand, between them and the house, lay sprawling untidily the dead bodies of three men, their male escorts, two laymen and a priest. This was a tight spot, and Alison knew it.

She had passed through Spain, after visiting Compostella, and had decided to go overland to Marseilles and thence by sea to Alexandria, instead of down Italy to Brindisi and by Malta and Rhodes, the more usual route, to visit Jerusalem again. She had done the Italian journey last time, and now wanted to see another country while she had the chance. So, like many other pilgrims, she had waited at Marseilles till she could find a company that suited her. Actually she had not much luck, for most pilgrims were taking the more usual route; and rather to her disgust she found herself having to join with a company of nuns. She had never liked nuns very much, and their boat was small and with only two seamen to man it, besides the priest in charge of the holy flock; and bad luck had followed them from the start. The seamen, indeed, had murmured that it was always unlucky to have nuns on board. A contrary wind had blown them back eastwards, right to within sight of Ceuta, and then a raking Moorish felucca had swept down on them, and a gang of murderous black men had hauled them off their little vessel and on to the other, landed them, sunk their little ship, and when the three men had put up a show of resistance, killed them. So here they were, eleven helpless women, at the mercy of their enemies.

Alison had tried talking to the Moors in such scraps of languages as she knew—a good deal of very indifferent dog-Latin, some tolerable French, a word or two of Spanish, and a phrase or two of Aramaic—but none of it seemed much use. They made signs, however, that the chief of the raiders was to go up to the big house, where it seemed that some great man lived, and that while he went, the prisoners were to wait.

So they had said their prayers together; and then Alison, feeling she had prayed as much as could reasonably be required of her, had retreated a little way from the rest of the party, and sat down on her own bundles, in the quiet and rather sinister sunshine, to await what might be going to happen.

Alison was now forty-seven; a fine sturdy frame of a woman, with the height to carry it, wide-hipped and deep-bosomed; her green eyes as lucent and full of sparkle as ever, her tawny hair parting off her well-proportioned forehead as sunnily as ever, her cheek as fresh, her lip as full. Much sunburning had freckled her, but never scalded her; and her waist remained trim, and her legs shapely. Many people would have called her ten years younger than she was.

And it looked likely enough that her life was to come to an end here, on the yellow desert, half way between Compostella and Jerusalem. At times like these, one meditates. . . .

The nuns, their office said, were filling in the time with readings from the Gospels. Far off, Alison could make out a veiled figure or two, like a picture from a Gospel letter—women fetching water from a well.

"And He said unto her, Thou hast well said, I have no husband, for thou hast had five husbands. . . ."

Five husbands. An odd passage for those nuns to be reading, as they crouched there, in terror for their virginities. Five husbands. Yes—Lucas, Watkyn, Harry, Baldwin, Jenkyn.

And if she were going to meet her Maker, perhaps in an hour?

Those nuns, now—would she be shamed before them? They would go straight into heaven, of course—the choice little white baa-lambs, brought up in the Church's innermost fold—or the preciously grown peaches, untouched, for the Master's own table . . . but she? Among the coarse common goats, surely . . .

And yet—they were still reading—"The Father seeketh such, to worship Him—"

Well! The dear Lord hadn't disdained the woman of Samaria—hadn't even taken her to task about her five husbands, though He knew all about them, even about the last one, who was "not thine husband." What then? Someone else's, or no husband to her—as a man could so easily be in more ways than one . . .

Oh, He hadn't criticized her, nor allowed those others to do so. There were things He understood, which those poor little nuns could never understand—

Five husbands, yes. And others besides. Oh, well—five in holy wedlock at the church door, and why not? That frightful old Lucas—Watkyn, poor kind man; roaring Harry, ah, he was a boy, in spite of all! Poor, meek, tamed old Baldwin, whom she used to torment so; and now Jenkyn, lovely wicked Jenkyn, delightful angel-faced devil, sitting back at home and getting into all sorts of mischief, spending all the money she had thought fit to leave with him, and then selling up every pewter pot in the house—ah, but the silver ones were all put away with Gamelyn, and all her other good stuff too, so that, waste as he might, there would be enough left for her boys though the Moors should cut her head off at sunset.

The sun was slanting downwards a little now, and over the sand she could see the men coming back. This was it. . . . There would be an ugly scene. The nuns, poor things, would sell their virginities dearly; they would resist and struggle, and the men would get impatient and rough, pull them about, knock them on the head to quiet them perhaps, and then lose their tempers altogether, and butcher them all, herself included. The old Mother Superior would fight like a tiger, and she hated to think what might be done to her . . . oh, it was going to be a nasty death and all so stupid—

The men came nearer, over the sandflats from the distant buildings. There were most of the original raiding party, and two other men, in rich robes—one a stooping man with a long, narrow grey beard nearly to his knees, a green turban, and a wand; the other walking behind him with a slow and stately step, a portly figure, so heavily muffled in a great cloak of red and white that they could see little of the man himself; from his dignity and attitude, evidently some great personage.

The nuns began to huddle together like sheep at the dog's approach, and Alison moved over to join them. She spoke to them in a low tone.

"Leave this to me. You have a chance—don't get excited. I'll see wha⁺ I can do."

They broke out in a terrified babble, but she silenced them with a gesture and walked out past them towards the oncoming men.

Within a few paces, the greybeard halted the party, and went on alone, the great man behind him. Then he stopped within arm's length of Alison, and addressed her in quite intelligible English. He told her that his master was the Bey of those parts, and that he was his interpreter and Vizier.

"Good day to your worships," said Alison, putting on her old bold face, though her heart sank as she looked at the group that stood before her. "I'm glad you speak English. Speak loud, though, for I'm hard of hearing. Commend me to your master, then, and what might he want?"

"These women," the Vizier replied, with a sweeping gesture. "All his. All women here, all his."

"No, no," Alison smiled confidingly. "Mine, if it please you, sir." She saw his bushy eyebrows lift enquiringly, and went on. "These women are all wives of His Holiness the Pope of Rome, and I am taking them as a present to his cousin the King of Jerusalem." Hastily she put up an inward prayer that the awful lie might be forgiven her, and added, "I am his chief bawd."

"So?" said the Vizier with interest. "But now they are all my master's." The Bey had come nearer, and had dropped his mantle from his face, showing himself to be a burly, hearty-looking coal-black man, with a beard even blacker and bushier than Harry's, and eyes that rolled in their white orbits.

Alison smiled politely, shook her head; then turned her looks to the Bey.

"Tell me," she said to the Vizier, "does your master want these women for himself or for his men? If, perhaps, he is a little too old—"

The Vizier looked more than a little affronted.

"The Bey? Too old? But no. He will have them for himself, he will not give them to his men."

"Indeed?" She looked the Bey up and down. He had begun to show interest, and appeared to be asking the Vizier what had been said. The Vizier translated, and turned back to her.

"He says—the King of Jerusalem will be disappointed."

"He will, without a doubt," said Alison, putting on a frown. "And very angry. These are some of His Holiness's best women. Moreover, they are all virgins." The last bit was true, anyway, she reflected. There was another pause, while rapid translation went on. The Bey's eye dwelt upon the black huddled forms, and then on her. As if in nervousness, she unfastened her wimple and her neckerchief, and allowed her red hair and the curve of her bosom to be seen. The Bey looked at her still more intently. But she turned to the Vizier.

"Tell me," she said, "is your master, then, a man of very great manhood?"

The Vizier grinned, and answered with enthusiastic gestures, much more eloquent than decorous.

"So? How many women will he ravish in a night?"

The Vizier grinned more widely, and counted on his fingers—on both hands. Alison shook her head, and laughed aloud.

"He will take one, and one only."

The Vizier looked shocked. The astonishing statement was relayed to the Bey—he grimaced, raising his great eyebrows, and laughed back.

"He says you lie, woman."

"Tell him I don't believe him." She took a few steps to and fro on the sand, flaunting herself. "Tell him he will take one, and one only, if I am she. Come now, a bargain. A wager. Tell your master."

The two men put their heads together, and jabbered—they were disturbed, intrigued, curious—the Bey was challenged and piqued. In the middle distance the nuns all turned their pale faces towards them, white circles against their black veils.

"What is your wager, woman?"

"Your master will take me first, this night—and if, after me, he wants one more of these, then let him take them all—I give them to him willingly." (Inwardly she was praying, Oh, holy Virgin, help me! I'm gambling with more than my own life.) "But if he is not able or desirous to take one more woman before sunrise, then let us all go on our way under safe conduct, by his oath on the Beard of the Prophet. Tell your master.

"A word more," said Alison. "You know, Your Worship, a woman can please a man or not please a man, as she chooses. Your master is not so ignorant of women but that he would rather have a willing one than an unwilling one, would he not?"

The Vizier nodded assent.

"Now, these—" Alison included them all with a sweep of her arm, "these are virgins. What are they? Green and unripe, narrow, bitter, like cucumbers. That is, the young ones—and the old ones, dried up and shrivelled—pickled in vinegar. Now I"—she flourished a rounded arm, bare above the elbow. "Ask your master what I am like."

Again, with broad grins, words were exchanged.

"He says—you are a ripe apricot."

"So be it! A ripe apricot against a basket of green cucumbers and old pickled gherkins! Will he play?"

The men muttered together. This was sheerest bluff, Alison knew. There was no reason at all why the Bey should make any bargain with her—they were all in his power anyway. Nor any reason why, once the bargain was made, he should keep it—but somehow she knew (remembering Ahmed) that this man would not break his word. She watched the two as they rumbled together—and suddenly they startled her with a gargantuan shout of laughter. The nuns heard it, and almost fainted.

"My master agrees, thou bold woman," said the Vizier. "You shall come to him first, and these others shall have safe and honourable shelter in his house till he sends for them. If he sends for one of them after you tonight, he has them all, and you too; but if not, you all go free before next sunset."

"You will feed and shelter them? And none of your men shall touch them?"

"Have no fear—the dogs do not touch their master's meat."

"He swears on the Beard of the Prophet?"

"On the Beard of the Prophet." And both the Vizier and the Bey laid their hands on their beards in the gesture Alison had learnt from Ahmed as being a binding oath.

"Agreed," she said and stretched out her right hand to the Bey, who took it in a hand surprisingly pleasant to the touch, being large, warm and gentle.

(But oh!—she prayed—Blessed Virgin, can you help me in this? It's not really your kind of affair, is it? After all, you wouldn't know—but oh, please, please, Mary Magdalene and Mary of Egypt, *you* might help me. . . .)

"Tell your women," said the Vizier, "and then come, we will take you to the house."

She hastened across the sand to them. They surrounded her with eager anxiety.

"It will be all right—I think," she told them, her voice dry with strain. "You are safe—I—hope. I am doing what I can for you." They pressed her with questions, but she told them nothing, as the robber band closed round them and led them towards the white walls that enclosed the house. They understood that in some way she was their sacrifice.

Inside the wall was a pleasant courtyard with fountains and palm trees, and even a few flowers; a few old Moorish women received them and led them away to bathe and feed. Then the Vizier appeared and parted Alison from them.

"Now, no tears," she told them, as they wept and prayed. "No, I can't tell you what I am going to do." She caught the eye of the old Mother Superior. "Reverend Mother—you understand—I'm not Judith . . . say rather I'm Esther for you. . . . Goodbye. Pray for me. It isn't going to be easy."

"God guard your chastity, dear friend," said one sweet little nun, clasping both her hands in hers.

"Thank you, dear." Alison kissed her forehead. (That, perhaps, is hardly what I need, she reflected—but at least I'll guard yours.) "Farewell—God keep you all," and the latticed door closed behind her.

Despite their anxiety, the nuns were so weary that they slept soundly. They were awakened to a sunny morning by Alison standing over them, her face radiant.

"All's well," she greeted them. "You're to go free today."

They scrambled to their feet, rubbing their eyes, dazed and incredulous, and overwhelmed her with questions.

"You are to have safe conduct, all your baggage back and beasts to carry it, and they will take you without fail to Alexandria and leave you there."

They broke into praises, falling on their knees, kissing rosaries and crucifixes.

"And—" gasped the youngest nun, all out for drama—"what of the Bey? Where is he? Did you kill him?"

"Not exactly," smiled Alison. "He is sleeping. But his Vizier will see you safely away—that's the old one with the long beard."

They renewed their alleluyas, praising Alison with the saints; she was their heroine, their martyr. How in the world had she done it?

"We must thank Saint Ursula in particular," said round-eyed little Sister Felicity.

"Why Saint Ursula?" asked the Mother Superior, arching her bushy old eyebrows rather quizzically.

"Oh, Saint Ursula had eleven thousand virgins," said Sister Felicity, "and anyhow, we're eleven virgins . . . I mean, there's ten of us, and—I mean . . ."

"Well, well! Five were wise and five were foolish, Sister Felicity," said the Superior, catching Alison's eye and seeing Alison's hand pressed to her mouth. A smile passed from the older woman to the younger.

"Break your fast, then," said Alison, as two swathed figures of indeterminate sex came in with bread, fruit and milk, "get your gear together, and be off. I will see you in Alexandria."

"What?" they chorused.

"I'm stopping here another week or so," she said, smirking. "I—well, I have more to do here." She led the Mother Superior aside to where the others could not hear.

"Me and the Bey's getting on like a house a-fire. He's a gentleman, for all that he's a heathen, and a proper man as ever was. He can't understand a word I say, and I'm too deaf to hear him, but it makes no odds. . . ."

Sister Felicity had another bright idea.

"Oh, Reverend Mother, is the Moor to be converted? Shall we see him baptized?"

Alison shook her head.

"Sister Felicity," said the Superior, "learn to be one of the five that were wise, and let well alone. Come, we'll thank God for our deliverance—oh, and Saint Ursula too if you wish—and get on our way."

Alison watched them out of sight from the wall of the fortress. Then she sat down on cushions under the palms, by the fountain, with a box of sweetmeats. The Bey was most unlikely to wake before sunset.

And so she came safely to Jerusalem for the third time, and worshipped in the Holy Sepulchre at yet another Easter. The nuns had of course got there before her, and greeted her with embarrassing praises. They wanted to publish her prowess all over Christendom, but the Mother Superior thought it better to restrain them. She was a woman of some sense, and she and Alison understood one another. She gathered from Alison that the Bey had learnt quite a few words of English in the three weeks or so that Alison had remained with him, but that the difficult matter of conversion had not been attempted. Sister Felicity was, of course, very disappointed; the others were perhaps more curious than anything, but they were doomed to disappointment also. Alison set off once more to Cyprus, across the Islands, and so to Venice.

And at Venice, going into the dim, cluttered, odorous warehouse of certain merchants with whom her brothers had alliance, to draw monies there deposited for her, she received a letter which had been left there many months before, when Adam's ship last touched there. It was a queer, brown bundle of stiff, creased parchment, wound round with silk and sealed with wax, and on it the impress of her son Gilbert's ring. She broke it open, and started to spell it out letter by letter, as best she might; but it was slow work, and in the end she was glad to ask the merchant's clerk to read it to her. The writing, all curlicues and flourishes, was none of Gilbert's, but dictated by him to his clerk as well. So it was read to her:

"Honourd Ladye when this doe come into your hand, know that I am well, and that at Whitt-Sunday last I took to wyffe Elizabeth Timmyng, daughter of mine hoost of the Devil and St Dunstan heere in Bristowe, which I doe hoope we doe have your blessing, the more that shee my wyffe is this day sevennight delivered of a daughter and booth well. We doe most hartely desire to see you, having as ever love and affection, whensoever it shall please you to returne, and so remain with duty and true piety, having you ever in my prayers, and to Allmighty God commending you, your son Gilbert.

"Given at mine own Shipyard on Severn Bank, this Piffany Sunday was three days."

Well, well—she lifted her eyes from the parchment, where she could make out, under the clerk's spidery tangles, the little private mark that was a sign between her and Gilbert. Little Gib married! Whitsun to Christmas—only seven months, the villain. Well, well—and a daughter, too. Good luck to her. She'd always wanted a daughter. And they desired to see her, did they? Suddenly like a physical pain she felt the longing to hold a baby at her breast again—a soft, pretty little girl-baby. And a great many other nostalgic longings came flooding back on her. England—yes, it was May now, and soon Italy would be too hot, but English meadows would be sweet and full of wild roses, as the swallows knew. Memories of sounds and smells assailed her. The trees, and the cawing rooks, and the soaked earth after rain. Two years she had been away—nearly three—and might have gone on without end, and not know that her son was wed and had made her a grandmother—

It was only secondarily that she thought of Jenkyn—but the thought of him pulled her heart, too. The dear, unbearable rascal! Where had he been adventuring? Had he forgotten her—or would he hold her in his arms again, and flatter and flirt and cozen her—

She lifted her eyes and stared straight before her; and then knew that she was staring at her own reflection. The dim little corner of the warehouse, the owner's sanctum, was a kind of small office, where he could interview clients, discount bills, show samples and sometimes sell ladies' jewellery—for which purpose a mirror hung on the wall; a rich Venetian mirror, bedight with gold and ebony, wide above and narrow below like a beautiful woman's face. And Alison was looking right into it, with a strong light coming down on her from an open loft above—and the face that looked back at her was older.

Lines here and lines there—a little coarsening of the texture, a sagging of the chin, the eyelids beginning to crumple like a withering flower, threads of grey through the tawny hair . . . oh, my God, this is what it looks like to be getting old? I'm a grandmother, too, a grandame, a beldame, a hag. No, I'm not, I'm Alison. . . . She felt her mouth go dry and her throat contract, and she turned away from the mirror with an angry gesture. Tcha! That old thief Time. Let it all go, and the Devil go with it. Time—high time to be getting home. Back to the fireside, comfort and quietude, and her grandchildren. But—there would still be Jenkyn. Oh yes—one man still to love and admire her, and treat her as a woman. Would he see the wrinkles and the grey hairs? Well and if he did—come now, the Bey hadn't minded a grey hair or two! That was six months ago, and she was still a ripe apricot. She would go back to Jenkyn before it was too late.

The little boat came tossing and bucketing along through the Bristol Channel and up into Severn mouth. How Alison loved the soft green English hills, the tiny fields, the hedges—all things she had missed. Coming home—it caught at her heart. Far off, as the boat drew in, she picked out her own house, its roof and its chimneys. Jenkyn would be there to meet her, with Gilbert and his Elizabeth. She wondered if Jenkyn would admire her new dress of Italian velvet. Jenkyn loved gay dresses.

They could see the crowd at the dockside now. Yes, there was Gilbert, and the girl by his side with the baby in her arms, that must be Elizabeth. They had seen her and were waving. But Jenkyn wasn't there. Well? No need to worry. He would be somewhere.

And at last, she was down the gang-plank and into Gilbert's arms. Bless him—he was so tall and broad, and so uncannily like his father. It was good to lay her head on his breast. But why were they all so subdued?

Almost before she could turn her attention to Elizabeth and her swaddled baby, she looked round for Jenkyn—and Gilbert and Elizabeth looked at each other.

"Shall we tell her? Yes—" But it had dawned on her.

"Jenkyn—I know—he's dead? Oh God—oh God's Mother—he's dead—"

"Yes, dear." Gilbert was so gentle, so tender, it unloosed her tears. "A month ago. A cold on the lungs. I'm—I'm sorry. God wot I never loved him, but—but *you* loved him—"

She broke down altogether and sobbed on Gilbert's breast without restraint.

"Come home, dearest. We'll take you. Come home and rest."

"Yes, yes, children," she wept, and her voice was weak and thin, 'take me home. I'm an old woman now—old and lonely. Take me home."

And they led her back to sit by the hearth in the shadows.

And so she remained, defeated and tired, through the winter. She had come to call herself an old woman, and her lovers and her friends were far from her. After the warm Mediterranean, she was surprised how the damp of England filled her with rheums and phlegms; her deafness increased, and her bones ached. This was not how she pictured England. For the first time in her life her hope had deserted her, and she was sorry for herself to the point of finality.

When she had been Lucas's slave, and the wretched bondmaid of his daughters—when she had been shunned by her neighbours after Watkyn's death—when Harry had terrified her day and night—she had had youth on her side and time before her—the pages of the book would turn, all things were in God's hands, and tomorrow would bring changes. But now, nothing could reverse old age and the damp, rotting hand of time. Before her lay only darkness and loss. Jenkyn was dead, kind godsib Alison was dead, and all her lusty paramours were gone into the dust.

Christmas might have roused her—she had always loved shows and plays, and here was all that she had been wont to delight in—and her three other sons came roaring home from sea, with money to spend and wine to lavish on her—but as bad luck would have it, she fell ill of a rheumy fever that kept her laid in bed almost the whole of Christmas time, and though she tried to rouse herself and enjoy the Christmas pies and the wassailing and murmuring, she made a poor hand of it. The rheum was settling in her ears, and she began to fear that she soon would not hear at all.

Then, as she began to recover from her sickness, she grew querulous, and would bustle about and interfere with Elizabeth's housekeeping—for Gilbert and Elizabeth had now taken over her house, so that they could look after her. She had plenty to do with her weaving business, which had never ceased to flourish, but that did not suffice her. Her temper was shorter than it had been, and as she herself grew harder of hearing, her voice grew louder. It maddened her when she couldn't hear what people said on the left side of her. Certainly her energy was coming back, but she had become a good bit of a trial to the household.

Until one day Gilbert said to her, "Mother, why don't you try another pilgrimage?"

PART THREE

PILGRIM'S REST

ONE

Absolution

"**WELL?**" she said, finishing the tale.

Chaucer stood up a trifle unsteadily. "*Confessio amantis,*" he said rather over-solemnly. "*Absolvo te—in nomine Veneris Cupidinisque. Quia multam amavit.*"

She shook her head. "I don't know much Latin, but that don't sound right. What's more, it sounds blasphemous to me. You oughtn't to say such things."

He shrugged his shoulders. "I'm a poet—we are allowed to be odd people. . . . Well, and so that's your story—and are you penitent?"

"Not a bit," she said stoutly. "Only—only sometimes when people talk—well, what's the good of all that—like these nuns and monks? Do you think we ought to keep our bodies saved up, like the talent hid in the earth, for—for what? To do what with 'em? To let 'em wither and rot? Tell me, why did the Lord

171

make us the way we are, the hes and the shes, if we were never to have the use of our bodies? Tell me that now!''

He shook his head at her. ''Oh, Alison, Alison, you mustn't disparage holy virginity. It is a very great grace.''

''I know, I know—God forbid I should say a word against a blessed virtue—why, I know that our Blessed Lord was a virgin-man, and He was the highest of all—but how could we all be that way, unless mankind were to come to an end? Why was a woman made to be a man's wife? Not to be a snare of the devil, that I'll never believe—that was the lies there was in that book of Jenkyn's, and I tore them out and burnt them.'' She chuckled a little over the recollection. Chaucer poured out the last cupful of wine, carefully dividing it between them.

''I tell you what,'' said Alison, ''it seems to me like this. The blessed saints and holy virgins—oh, I know there's some of them, they're not all like that Prioress—well, the holy virgins are the pure white wheaten bread that the priest takes for the blessed wafers. But we wives, we're barley bread—but didn't the good Lord make a multitude of men happy with a few barley loaves?''

''Five thousand, my Alison—and the bread though never so much divided was enough for them all.''

''Well, I'd enough for them all. Not five thousand, only five—oh, and others . . .''

''Never mind the others.''

''I remember when I saved the virginity of those ten nuns, and one of them, bless her, tried to make it eleven thousand like Saint Ursula. Well, God wot I didn't have five thousand husbands—but wasn't I bar-

172

ley bread for a good many?—Of course I suppose it's better to be the wheaten bread—"

"Without doubt, my dear, it is the way of perfection."

"Without doubt it is . . . ."

"And don't you want to be perfect?"

She pondered a minute, and then with her eyes wide with candour, said, "No."

"Oh, Alison!" cried Chaucer, with a gust of astonished laughter, flinging his arms round her, "you're a nonesuch!"

And far away in her memory, she caught an echo.

He kissed her heartily, and then immediately grew grave and rather embarrassed, and drew away from her.

"Pardon—don't know how I came to do such a thing—mustn't let Philippa know—meant nothing by it, my dear, nothing at all."

And that was true, thought Alison with some surprise. Here she had talked with this man all night, liked him with all her heart, yet not loved him, nor wished him to desire her; and they had talked almost as man to man, yet not quite—a remote flirtation of the spirit. A new experience and a pleasant one.

"God's my life, it's daybreak," she said. "Well, I'm not going up *there*. They'll think the worst of me anyway—let them think. I don't owe them any money. Hey-ho, I'm sleepy. I shall sleep in the saddle all day. Good-night—well, good-morning, then, Master Chaucer. It's been good—oh, by the Mass, I'm near asleep now. I'll walk the lanes till breakfast-time."

He watched her out of sight, thoughtful. He was more than sleepy himself.

TWO
The Sign

THE pilgrimage drew towards its end.

It was the fourth night—the next day would see them all in Canterbury. All the tales were told, and it had been agreed that the Parson should have the floor tomorrow, and preach them into Canterbury with a holy discourse—to prepare them to approach the shrine of the blessed saint by washing out of their minds all recollections of the naughtier stories. And some had been very naughty indeed.

It had turned warm—the day had been brilliant, and now the evening was lingering and mild, full of the scent of elder and currant-bushes and hawthorn; the sky still glowed, and the moonlight would take over before the daylight faded. The company, having supped, sat sprawling on benches before the inn door, or strolled to and fro along the white dusty lanes. It was too hot for sleep.

Mostly the company had strayed off in twos and threes, but Alison walked alone, pondering, summing up her ride. It had been a pleasant four days, and the stories had been a great idea and most successful. She was glad she had come, for all that she had not yet so far found a sweetheart. There were possibilities . . . the Lawyer, the Knight and the Franklyn were widowers, the Squire of course a bachelor, as were also the Clerk, the Doctor, and—probably—the Shipman. The rest were married, except for the clerics, and she didn't count clerics. Harry Bailey, the Host, was a man after her own heart, but goodness knows he was married, and to a shrew. Even if Alison had been minded to try to steal a man from his wife—a thing she would not do—there was no entering into competition there. She liked the Knight, and he had been very attentive to her; a more charming and courteous man you couldn't meet, and at mealtimes, and at casual halts by the wayside for the odd can of ale, he had paid her small attentions and hovered by her, with his gentle voice and his blue eyes. . . . It would be wonderful to be a Knight's lady! They had something in common, too—he could talk with her about the Holy Land, and Italy, and Africa, and Constantinople—moreover, finding she understood such talk, he told her about other places where she hadn't been—Bohemia, and Muscovy. . . . His son didn't like it, though—she could see him watching them, uneasy, impatient, and red in the face. Yes, that would be a complication. A nice young fellow—oh, a very nice young fellow—but as a stepson—?

The Franklyn intrigued her, and she would have liked to see more of him. There seemed a perverse fate that prevented her from ever encountering him close at hand or for long—so that she still hadn't solved the puzzle of who it was he reminded her of. She hadn't even heard his tale, for the Prioress had taken that moment to protest against the arrangement by which Alison always rode at the narrator's left—and had threatened such a fuss that Alison was asked by all of them to change places with her for once. So she never heard the Franklyn's tale of Dorigen, which was a pity, for it was a good one. No matter—perhaps she would make his acquaintance better on the way back; for to make his acquaintance she was determined.

There was also, of course, Master Chaucer the poet—queer little fellow, whom she liked almost as much as any she had met—but somehow, not as a sweetheart. It would be extremely pleasant and good, she felt, to have this wise little man as her true and confidential friend, a thing she had not known since she lost her godmother Alison. She wondered what he had made of that farrago of truth and exaggeration she had told him over a blackjack of Xeres sack two evenings past. . . .

Down the deepening, wooded lane she was pacing in meditation. There were high turfy banks, where the rabbits had only lately ceased springing; and crouched above, dwarfish bushes of thorn and juniper took fantastic shapes in the dim light. First the path was open to the moonlight, then it plunged into a tunnel of dark boughs.

And a man stepped out before her.

She checked a scream as soon as she saw it was one of the company. It was the Summoner—and as she looked at him her heart began to thud with fright again. Black and shaggy, with his swollen, red, pimpled face, smelling of liquor and garlic, with another great garland of flowers round his ugly head as in mockery—he was an unpleasant sight. She stood her ground, however.

"Mistress Johnson—no, don't run away. All alone? Come now, that won't do. *Femme sole* should be *femme couverte*—don't you think so?"

"As you say, Master Summoner," she answered rather falteringly, not knowing at all what to answer. She was annoyed with herself that she should be afraid of this man—after all, she knew the worst and best of men by now, and she was no shrinking virgin—what was there to be afraid of? But she was afraid of him, horribly afraid.

"Questio quid juris." He rolled his tongue round the meaningless words. "Come a bit closer to me, my dear. I like your looks, by God's boots! You're the kind of woman a man could go for. You're not afraid of me either. Come here, I say."

She tried to keep a grip on the situation.

"Thank you very much, Master Summoner—I would rather not, so please you."

"Rather not!" His voice thickened with anger. "Rather not! Do you know who you are talking to? *In ecclesiam sanctam*—woman, I can have you to the archdeacon's court for your sins—adultery, seduction, incest, and corruption of the young—"

"You old devil, stop talking nonsense!" she fired back at him. "You can't accuse me of any of those things, and I'm not in your diocese anyway—"

"No? Then shut your mouth, you harlot," he growled, and pouncing like a cat, seized her brutally. His foul great lips pressed down upon hers, robbing her of breath. She fought, desperately—after a minute freeing her mouth from his, she screamed aloud. A shout answered her, and the sound of running feet. The Summoner let go of her, and pelted down the path; and she collapsed against the leather-clad shoulder of her rescuer, the Knight.

With the very tenderest care he soothed and settled her, anxiously enquired if she were hurt, supported her with a firm arm, gazing down into her dilated eyes.

"That Summoner!" she burst out. "The lewd, nasty, scald-headed knave—the canting holy hypocrite—the rotten blackmailer—as drunk as a fiddler, he is—"

The Knight shook his head and smiled sadly.

"It's a pity to see a man go that way. Maybe he was a good man once."

"Oh, Sir Knight!" she retorted. "I believe you'd find a good word for the devil himself. Bless you, you've neither guile nor gall in you. But there's plenty of naughty rogues in the world."

"I can't revile them, though I fight them. All men are men, and—hard words don't come easily off my tongue. Yet I haven't forgiven that man for affrighting you."

They stood together in the moonlight, a blossoming elder-tree shedding fragrance over them. His hands rested lightly on her shoulders.

"Mistress Alison—I feel as if I had known you longer than these four days. You are—I should say—I mean—I have never known a lady so amiable as you. My dear wife, who is with God, was a great lady and very handsome, but—not like you. Mistress—dear Mistress Alison—could you love me?"

Her heart leapt. This was crazy, but what a rich

prize within her grasp. This charming, sweet-voiced gentleman, with money and the name of lady to offer her—his generous heart shining in his innocent blue eyes—why not say yes, and seize her advantage? Why not?—Because of a sound coming along the further lane below them that made her stiffen and draw back. A young man's voice, singing aloud and idly in a clear high tenor.

"Sir Knight," she said, demurely and yet with a little touch of affectionate warmth, "you honour me, and yet—I'll say, no thank you. There's one coming that it wouldn't suit. Pray you, as you're a wise man, leave me now, and let him not see us together. I—thank you a thousand times for—everything—and part good friends."

She held out her hand. He took it, repeating, "And part good friends." Then quickly—for he too had heard the approaching voice—he lifted the hand to his lips, and was gone.

She was still standing quiet under the elder-tree when the Squire came past.

"Why, Mistress Alison, you're abroad late. The lights are out at the inn."

"You're late yourself, Master Leonard. A growing boy like you should be in his bed."

He made an impatient gesture.

"A growing boy! I'm a man, if they'd let me be one. And I can't sleep. Who can, on a night like this?"

She smiled at him. He was picturesquely dishevelled—his uncovered golden hair tossed about, his flowered doublet open at the neck.

"What's the matter, my poor lad? Are you in love?"

He gave a groan that was not altogether insincere.

179

"One's always in love—but this time, this is the real thing. I'm dying of it, Mistress Alison, dying of it. D'you wonder I can't sleep?"

She fell into step beside him and paced with him a little further along the lane. All had fallen very quiet now, and far off in distant woods there were nightingales singing.

"Do you mock me, Mistress Alison? You who have had so much experience, you who know all the old dance of love, do you think me a fool?"

She sighed.

"Never in my life, dear boy. God forbid I should ever mock a lover. Why do you think I should?"

He turned half round at her side, and contemplated her. This was the woman he had been thinking hardly of, resenting his father's attention to her, looking on her as bold and unscrupulous. But she was different. Perhaps it was the light—?

She was speaking again.

"You think hardly of me. You have been rating me as an enemy."

He caught his breath.

"Good God! Are you a sorceress, that you read my thoughts?"

"No, no, lad—only a woman who knows a little of the hearts of men. I know you have been afraid of me, because you thought your father the Knight would marry me. Put that thought away from you, boy—he's asked me within this hour, and I said no and I mean no. There you are. Now you can trust me."

"Oh—" he said, deeply and overcome, and found it hard for a few minutes to say any more. Then:

"Why did you do that—dear lady?"

"Why?—Why indeed?"

They had stopped again, this time under a giant beech at whose foot the bluebells bloomed. She faced him, and his arm stole round her shoulders. Gazing into her face, he hardly saw her nearly fifty years. The magnetism of her personality reached out to him and pulled him, and for a moment he had quite forgotten his far-away, cold and scornful love. She, his adored, could be an iceberg if she wished—but here was warmth and radiance, and a breast where a man could lay his head and remember his mother. . . .

She went on speaking gently, in that whisper which seemed natural to the moonlit night.

"Because I didn't want you to have me for a step-mother."

"A stepmother?" He laughed. "No, no—that's no good. I don't want a stepmother. But, Alison, darling Alison—supposing I said—not a stepmother, but—"

"But what, sweet lad?"

"But my lovely sweetheart—"

She let his lips meet her own. The touch of them was like sweet fresh fruit. For a moment she let herself enjoy that kiss. Then she put him gently from her.

"No, my dear. It can't be. I'm an old fool, and you're—a young darling. I mustn't steal you. This is a dream, and you will wake in the morning."

Reluctantly he released her.

"Go back to your bed now, and dream of your own mistress. And when you marry her, call one of your children Alison."

Without a word, he kissed her hand as his father had done, and walked slowly away. His receding footsteps echoed in the quiet woods; and Alison stood listening, leaning against the beech, while two great tears spilled from her eyelids and rolled down over her cheeks.

It was upon her right that the footsteps went away; so she did not hear Master Chaucer, stealing up on her left.

"Oh—" she gasped. "You crept up on me like—an elf."

"Come," he said softly and mysteriously, laying one hand on her arm, and the finger of the other on his lips. "No words—come. I bring you a sign."

"A sign? A sign of what?"

But he made no answer.

He led her a few steps on, into the wood; there was a bent birch-tree overhanging a gap, and he held it back, at the same time gently restraining her from going forward.

Before her was a little enclosed greensward, bright in the moonlight. She looked intently.

"I see nothing," she said.

Chaucer laid one hand lightly on her head. "Look again," said his quiet voice.

And then she saw them, as she had seen them once before in her childhood—the tiny dancers.

Glimmering white and green they moved, exquisite, translucent, no more than a span high—men and women, perfect and delicate, but too far away and small to see more than their dainty outlines and movements—passing and turning, round and round, up and over, lightly as motes in a sunbeam. Yes, just as she remembered them, once before. One night when she had gone out with Gamelyn, coney-catching. When she was young and a maid—before all this had happened to her. Right at the beginning of things.

She watched them, hardly daring to breathe. Their beauty was beyond this world, and so was their sweet happiness. While one could count a hundred she watched them, and then a breeze stirred the leaves—though the night was windless—and they were gone.

Master Chaucer let the branch swing back again like a curtain. She turned to face him.

"Oh—what does it mean? What does it mean?"

"I don't know, my dear—how should I know? But it's a sign for you."

"A sign of what? Of my death?—Some people say you die if you see them. . . ."

"No, why should it be a sign of death? But a sign it surely is. Trust God, and goodnight."

He patted her on the shoulder, and without another word went swiftly down the path away from her. She passed her hand over her brow, sighed deeply, and went slowly back to the inn.

THREE

Miracle at Canterbury

THE great day had come, and they were in Canterbury. They had ridden leisurely from breakfast-time onwards, listening to the good Parson's solemn discourse; then before the sun was at noon, they had ridden in through the gates of Canterbury, joined on all sides by other pilgrims, and had sung a hymn under the gateway. The streets were bustling and gay, and the bells rang out. This was Saturday, and they would make their devotions to Saint Thomas after the midday meal, and on Sunday hear High Mass.

First, then, they settled themselves at the hostel, changed their clothes and dined. All were somewhat strung up and anxious, and did not talk much. The relaxation and good cheer would come at supper afterwards, when each one's vow had been paid, and perhaps—perhaps there would be miracles of healing.

Perhaps the Summoner's pimples would clear—perhaps old Oswald the Reeve would be cured of his dry hacking cough—perhaps Alison would get her hearing fully restored. The Knight was seriously bent on returning thanks for his deliverance after the foreign wars—the Shipman, though not quite so serious, had thanks to make as well, for deliverance from the sea, and had brought a little model to give to the shrine; it represented his ship the *Maudelayne,* and he had carved it beautifully with his own hands. He also hoped it would bring him luck in future voyages. The Pardoner, of course, hoped for trade, and that would be no miracle.

By about two of the Cathedral clock they were all ready, formed up in a long procession with the other pilgrims, beginning to pace slowly, slowly into the Cathedral. All had changed into the better clothes they had brought with them, except for the Parson, the Ploughman, and the Clerk, who had brought none, but walked modestly and had no eyes for display. The Prioress was resplendent in a snowier mountain of linen than ever before—she must have persuaded the women at the inn to launder for her, for that wimple and gorget had never come like that out of a saddle-bag. But still she had the dogs all round her, and spent the time of waiting vigorously brushing them. Most of them were on a multiple lead, but the favoured Sweeting ran free, and got in everyone's way. The Nun had to keep on attending to them and rounding them up.

It was a brilliantly hot day, and the procession sweltered patiently in the sun, moving up step by step. Alison found it far from tedious; there were so many other pilgrims to look at, in the long zigzag line that countermarched across the space before the great west door—there were the wonderful carvings on the huge west front of the Cathedral—and if that failed, the memory of so many other pilgrimages to recall. But of course she ought to be praying. So ought they all, though quite manifestly some of them were not. With compunction, Alison drew a rosary from her pocket, and tried to concentrate on it. She was to pray very hard, she reminded herself, and perhaps Saint Thomas would give her back the hearing of her left ear. Although now, it was true, amid the sunshine and liveliness, her partial deafness seemed of less importance than it had been in the winter, when it had been the ever growing centre of her depression. She could make a shift, no doubt, to live as she was—she had got used to it—but how did she know what sounds she might have become accustomed to missing? At that moment, it was only by turning her head right round that she could perceive that the monks were singing in the Cathedral. Sweet, high, lovely music, and when she straightened her head, she missed it all. And if the rheums made it worse in the winter, and she a lonely old woman by the fireside, unable to hear tales or songs at all . . . Oh well—blessed Saint Thomas, *ora pro nobis, ora pro nobis . . . please . . .*

The Prioress was just in front of her, with the Nun and of course the dogs, and her obsequious priest, whispering discreetly and courteously from time to time; next beyond them she could see the Franklyn, still as elusive and intriguing to her as ever. Old Daisy-beard, she called him to herself—the neat little white beard she could just see if he happened to turn his head—it was newly-trimmed, and his close-cropped silvery hair had a gloss of vigorous health and cleanliness about it. An adequate, well-found man, capable and cheerful—she hoped he would not fail to remain with the party on the return journey.

And so in due turn they passed out of the sunlight into the great and awesome wonder of the Cathedral; and the singing of the monks was all around them. The coloured windows shed their glory, and the great pillars welcomed them. Far ahead and up a long flight of steps was a glow of candles, which was the shrine of pilgrimage. The whole company joined in the hymn—here and there were some that prayed aloud—a hysterical woman shrieked and was carried out in a fit—sometimes a resounding outcry was raised as someone felt they had received healing. The pace of the procession quickened as they began to ascend the stone steps, already worn blunt by so many feet.

It would appear that the Powers Above, to whom these things are delegated by Higher Authority, have a liking for bathos.

Sweeting was not, as has been mentioned before, house-trained; and there was evidence of that fact on the step where Alison, her eyes upward and dreaming, set her foot. She slipped forward, fell, and her head struck the stone step before her with a shattering impact. They thought she was dead. . . .

She came up out of the darkness, to hear voices, clear as never before, singing, and a voice she recognized calling her by her name. Without opening her eyes she spoke.

"Heaven," she said. "Dear blessed God, it's heaven! How did you find me, Gilbert?"

Then she opened her eyes, and saw the face of the Franklyn bending over her, and knew it was his arms that held her.

"It *is* Gilbert!" she cried. "Gilbert, my love and my sweet, do you know me? You—you called me by my name, and I knew your voice." And she raised her face to his and kissed him. It had not dawned on her yet that they were in the middle of a crowd. "I knew your voice—why—why—*I can hear plainly!*"

She lay back gasping with delight, although everything was still whirling round her. She was lying where she had fallen on the steps, with the pilgrims anxiously clustered round her, and Gilbert—yes, Gilbert her sweetheart of years ago—was supporting her in his arms. She felt his hold tighten, and knew she had not been mistaken.

"Why, my little girl of the woods—is it you indeed? My darling—" And his voice, the deep purring voice which in her deafness she had found so hard to hear, shook with tenderness.

And the word ran up and down the line and through the Cathedral like wildfire—"A miracle! A miracle of healing! The Wife of Bath's deafness is cured, before she ever got to the shrine! Praise be to God and to Saint Thomas!"

And in the meantime Sweeting, the unconscious instrument of the miracle, had been speeded out of the procession by a well-aimed kick of the Franklyn's foot, and was flying for refuge to the horse-lines, where he rewarded himself with some poorer pilgrim's supper-basket.

But Alison rose to her feet on the Franklyn's arm and came up the steps, shaken but completely happy. Here were two miracles. And he, for his part, held her firm and warmly, and was more content with the choice that fortune had made for him.

*   *   *

So the rest of the stories remained untold, and
Alison's own story is soon finished.

That very Sunday she and the Franklyn were married in the Cathedral, having first given thanks in
public, with all the congregation, for a great and nota-
ble miracle; and she returned home with him to his fine
house in Norfolk, where the tables stood laid all day
and it snowed meat and drink. They travelled by themselves, and let company alone; and their going broke
up the party, who returned in ones and twos among
other parties. Cook Roger's ulcer was cured too,
though this hardly got as much publicity as Alison's
healing; Reeve Oswald's cough was much better
thenceforward; but the Summoner's face remained as
bad as ever it was, like his conscience. Chaucer and
the Doctor had long and learned confabulations and
took multitudinous notes; and Chaucer, moreover,
gave Alison in marriage to the Franklyn, and kissed
her solemnly, and promised to visit her in Norfolk. As
to the Prioress, she primmed up her lips and said that
Providence doubtless knew its own ways best, but,
well, as if *five* husbands weren't enough! Harry Bailey
rode back to his quarrelsome wife, and thought of
Alison with regret. And the Knight's son, when at last
he did marry (but it was a different lady, some ten
years later) did call his first born daughter Alison.

And as to whether Alison and Gilbert lived happily
ever after—well, certainly they had every reason to do
so. Let it suffice that she never had another husband,
nor he another wife. Sometimes she used to think that
if only Gilbert had been her first husband, as he was
her first lover, she need never have had the

others—but then, of course, she would have missed so many things. Hanging and wiving, as godmother Alison often said, go by destiny; and Alison had fulfilled her destiny, and was well content.

THE HISTORY-MAKING
#1 BESTSELLER
ONE YEAR ON
THE NEW YORK TIMES LIST!

THE THORN BIRDS

COLLEEN McCULLOUGH

AVON 35741 $2.50